"Mega... Brian's Na...

Megan's face we...

Holt supposed he... it out. "A few months ago, my son became very curious about his biological parents. The attorney who handled the adoption died several years ago, but the investigator I hired managed to track you down."

Megan's mouth dropped open. "This is crazy! I gave birth to a *girl*, Mr. Ramsey. And if my baby had lived, I would *never* have given her up for adoption."

Holt was shocked. "But Brian's crazy about you." *And so am I.*

"I like him, too, but I'm not his mother. This is all some stupid mistake."

"Are you *sure* it's a mistake?" he asked. "I have some pretty convincing evidence...."

Dear Reader,

Welcome once again to Silhouette Desire! Enter into a world of powerful love and sensuous romance, a world where your most passionate fantasies come true.

September begins with a sexy, sassy MAN OF THE MONTH, *Family Feud* by Barbara Boswell, a writer you've clearly indicated is one of your favorites.

And just as exciting—if you loved Joan Johnston's fantastic HAWK'S WAY series, then don't miss CHILDREN OF HAWK'S WAY, beginning with *The Unforgiving Bride*.

The month is completed with stories from Lass Small, Karen Leabo, Beverly Barton and Carla Cassidy. *Next* month, look for a MAN OF THE MONTH by Annette Broadrick *and* the continuation of Joan Hohl's BIG, BAD WOLFE series.

So, relax, read, enjoy…and fall in love all over again with Silhouette Desire.

Sincerely yours,

Lucia Macro
Senior Editor

Please address questions and book requests to:
Silhouette Reader Service
U.S.: 3010 Walden Ave., P.O. Box 1325, Buffalo, NY 14269
Canadian: P.O. Box 609, Fort Erie, Ont. L2A 5X3

KAREN LEABO
MEGAN'S MIRACLE

SILHOUETTE *Desire*®
Published by Silhouette Books
America's Publisher of Contemporary Romance

SILHOUETTE BOOKS

ISBN 0-373-05880-2

MEGAN'S MIRACLE

Copyright © 1994 by Karen Leabo

This edition published by arrangement with Harlequin Enterprises B. V.

® and TM are trademarks of Harlequin Enterprises B. V., used under
license. Trademarks indicated with ® are registered in the United States
Patent and Trademark Office, the Canadian Trade Marks Office and in
other countries.

Printed in U.S.A.

Books by Karen Leabo

Silhouette Desire

Close Quarters #629
Lindy and the Law #676
Unearthly Delights #704
The Cop #767
Ben #794
Feathers and Lace #824
Twilight Man #838
Megan's Miracle #880

Silhouette Romance

Roses Have Thorns #648
Ten Days in Paradise #692
Domestic Bliss #707
Full Bloom #731
Smart Stuff #764
Runaway Bride #797
The Housewarming #848
A Changed Man #886

KAREN LEABO

credits her fourth-grade teacher with initially sparking her interest in creative writing. She was determined at an early age to have her work published. When she was in the eighth grade she wrote a children's book and convinced her school yearbook publisher to put it in print.

Karen was born and raised in Dallas. She has worked as a magazine art director, a free-lance writer and a textbook editor, but now she keeps herself busy full-time writing about romance.

One

"Mr. Ramsey?"

The receptionist's soft voice captured Holt's attention. He looked up from the magazine he'd been pretending to read. "Yes?"

"Would you like to speak with one of the other designers?"

"No," he replied too quickly, too emphatically. "I have to see Ms. Carlisle. She came so highly recommended, I...I really want to work with her."

The young receptionist smiled benignly. "I hate to make you wait forever. I expected Ms. Carlisle to be back in the office long before now. Perhaps you'd like to make an appointment with her for later in the week?"

"I don't mind waiting," he said, although he minded very much. Still, it was his own fault for impulsively dropping in at NuWorld Kitchen Designs the moment he discovered Megan Carlisle worked there. He'd been sitting in this

damned uncomfortable chair for almost an hour, and he
would wait another hour if he had to, as long as there was
the possibility that Ms. Carlisle could walk in at any moment. He hated to admit it, but his curiosity was getting the
better of him.

Would she be anything like the snooty little rich girl the
private investigator's report had described? Holt was a bit
surprised to find her actually holding a job, but maybe she'd
grown bored with shopping and volunteer work. Maybe this
wasn't even a real job, but something more of a courtesy, a
convenient place to stash a divorced society girl who was too
old to live with her mother but too incompetent to actually
support herself. The man who owned NuWorld moved in
important Dallas social circles. Perhaps he had given Ms.
Megan Carlisle a token job as a favor to her mother or
something. Here, she could play with color samples and
pretend she was being useful.

Holt hadn't seen any pictures of Megan Carlisle, with the
exception of one group shot of her debutante class, and that
one was grainy and indistinct. He wondered if she would
look like Brian.

Holt tugged at the collar of his polo shirt. The late-
summer Texas sun streamed in through a double skylight,
and the waiting room was sweltering. Either that, or he was
more nervous than he thought. He supposed he had a right
to be nervous. After months of searching, he was about to
come face-to-face with the woman who had given birth to
his son. He wouldn't go so far as to refer to her as Brian's
mother. Shelley, Holt's wife, had been Brian's mother, pure
and simple.

The outer door opened and a woman entered, her arms
filled with sample books, legal pads and manila folders. A
huge black leather portfolio dangled from one dainty wrist,

and an overflowing shoulder bag hung at her elbow, having obviously slipped from her shoulder where it belonged.

"What a morning!" she exclaimed, peeking over the top of the precariously balanced armload. Holt could just make out the velvety brown eyes peering through a fringe of dark bangs. "First I had to drive all the way to Fort Worth to show that numskull Mrs. Aylesworth the new blueprints, which she *still* had problems with, and then there was a hellacious wreck on the turnpike. I thought I never would—"

She halted as the receptionist cleared her throat and gestured frantically. "Megan, this gentleman is here to see you."

She turned her doe's eyes on him, and his mouth went dry. Anger welled up inside him, but the feeling was tempered with something else. The sudden weakness in his knees and the tightness in his gut—feelings that had nothing to do with animosity—were totally unexpected and not at all welcome.

Megan stuck out her right hand and offered a tentative smile. "Hi, I'm Megan Carlisle." As she made the gesture, she upset the precarious balance of her stack, and the folders on top cascaded one by one to the floor, spreading their contents in a noisy shower of papers. Reflexively, Holt made a grab for the last folder and caught it as the receptionist jumped up from behind her desk to gather up the mess, muttering something about unmade beds.

He set the folder on top of the stack, right about chin level, then took Megan's outstretched hand. It was soft and warm. "Holt Ramsey."

"Nice to meet you. Here, would you mind?" Without waiting for his reply, she thrust two large sample books toward him, revealing more of the woman who'd been hidden behind them. He scanned her face and body for signs of Brian, but he detected nothing in common between this mischievous pixie and his tall, angular son. Not more than five foot two, she had a gamin face that included a sprinkling of freckles across her straight, patrician nose. While Brian's hair was black, hers was a deep chocolate brown that flew in all directions as she spun around to lead him out of the reception area, presumably to her office.

The receptionist ran after them. "Megan, you forgot your messages." She tossed a handful of pink slips on top of the books Holt carried, gave him an apologetic smile and scurried back to her desk.

"Sorry, my office is a long way back here. That's where they stick the drones like me, the ones who haven't earned any seniority. I've only been here a few months. So, what can I do for you Mr.... Dang, I already forgot your name."

"Ramsey." Holt could have answered her question in a number of different ways. What he wanted, at the moment, was to touch her again and see if her body was as soft as it looked in her lavender silk T-shirt and matching pants. The outfit was casual but professional, and it molded to the curves of her body in just the right places.

This cheerful imp of a woman had taken him completely by surprise. He had expected someone tall and cool who would look down her nose at him, someone who would call her lawyer the moment she found out her son was looking for her—just to make sure she wasn't liable for anything. He couldn't imagine *this* Megan Carlisle even having a lawyer.

Still, appearances could be deceiving. He didn't plan to give her a hint of the true reason he'd come to call until he had thoroughly investigated her character. He wouldn't allow her contact with Brian until he was sure she wouldn't hurt him. The boy had handled enough pain for one young lifetime.

Megan, her arms still overflowing despite the pile Holt had taken on, stooped so that she could twist the doorknob to her office. Then she wedged the door open with one dainty foot and flipped on the lights with her elbow.

"Just set that stuff anywhere," she said as she dropped her armful onto the floor.

Holt followed suit, as there didn't seem to be anywhere else to deposit the sample books and folders. Every available surface in the small office, including Megan's desk, drawing board, credenza, bookshelves and both chairs, was covered with stack upon stack of stuff similar to what he had just carried in. A filing cabinet, both doors open, bristled with sticky notes peeking from various folders. He saved the phone messages from what he guessed would be permanent oblivion by setting them on the desk.

Without much concern, Megan moved a box of paint chips from her chair and sat down, taking a deep breath. "Oh, just throw that stuff on the floor," she said breezily when she saw him looking with irritation at the only other chair in the room. "Sorry the place is such a wreck. With the number of jobs I have running through here, I need an office three times this size with floor-to-ceiling shelves, but I can't seem to convince my boss of that. At least I know pretty much where everything is."

Holt cleared off the chair and sat, moving slowly as he wondered what he would say to her. He supposed there was no choice except to feign interest in a new kitchen. "I hear you design some nice kitchens," he said, careful to screen out all emotion from his voice. "I'd like to get your ideas on remodeling mine."

Her smile lit up the whole room. "You mean, someone actually referred you to me? Who was it?"

"I sort of overheard your name at a party. They said you were very good at what you do." He tried not to grimace at telling such a blatant lie. Megan Carlisle was probably a disaster. Otherwise, why would she be so surprised that someone had recommended her?

"How nice! I haven't had time to complete very many jobs. I have quite a few in progress, but most clients aren't satisfied until everything is in place and the workers are gone. Before that, they think it's just a big pain in the—" She stopped herself. "Gosh, I hope I haven't just talked you out of remodeling."

"I haven't actually been talked *into* doing it yet," he told her. "I'll need to find out more about it."

"Great! Let's get started, then. I have more than an hour before I have to leave for another appointment." As she talked, she cleared a space on her desk and produced a leather-bound notebook, an expensive-looking fountain pen and a calculator. "That's Holt, H-O-L-T, right?"

"That's right."

She paused, her pen poised above her lavender legal pad. "I'm hungry."

"What?"

"I just realized this is my lunch hour, and it's probably yours, too. Why don't we do this over sandwiches? There's a great deli right around the corner." Without giving Holt a chance to object, she popped out of her chair, grabbed up her things along with her purse and a handful of glossy brochures and nodded toward the door, indicating that he should precede her.

He really didn't want to turn this meeting into a social occasion, but she didn't give him much choice. "What about your phone messages?" he reminded her.

"What? Oh, yeah, I guess I should at least take a look at them. I'm sure they're mostly from vendors, and they don't expect me to call back in any timely manner." She set down her things, picked up the stack of pink slips and flipped through them without much interest...until she reached the last one. Then she smiled again, wistfully this time. "Heather. I wonder what she wants," Megan murmured.

"Who?" he asked automatically.

"Oh, um, just an old friend from high school. Haven't talked to her in years. I'll call her later." She set the messages aside and headed for the door, apparently carefree, but there was a certain stiffness to her shoulders, a thoughtfulness to her expression—and yes, even vulnerability—that Holt hadn't seen before. For the first time, he saw something beyond the facade of the slightly ditzy whirlwind she'd unknowingly presented herself as.

Over the top of her ice tea glass, Megan stared at her new client. He was about six feet tall, a respectable, clean-cut sort, with medium brown hair combed back from a high forehead and trimmed neatly around his ears. His eyes, a deep smoky blue, reflected intelligence. His other features were a bit too sharp to be called handsome, but the overall impression was strikingly masculine.

Despite his impeccable manners, she sensed an undeniably earthy streak, a dangerously potent sexuality underlying his more civilized veneer.

The combination gave her an unexpected thrill. He appeared to be single, or at least there was a good possibility he was, since he hadn't mentioned a wife and didn't wear a ring. As he'd sat across from her in the office, her imagination had run wild even as she had tried to conduct business. It had been a long time—too long—since the mere look of a man, the gleam in his eye and the sound of his voice had affected her so.

Realizing how hazardous her speculations could be, she took a dainty bite of her sandwich and forced her thoughts onto other avenues...like that message from Heather Shipman.

Heather, her best friend from high school, her confidante, the one she'd turned to when she'd found out she was pregnant. Heather, whose friendship had withered for lack of attention. In her pain and grief, Megan had turned away from all of her friends. They wouldn't have understood.

Reading her name scrawled across the pink slip of paper, Megan had felt the oddest stab of nostalgia for the friend she'd lost. After more than fourteen years, what could Heather possibly want?

"Don't you like your sandwich?"

Megan was brought abruptly back to the present by the sound of Holt Ramsey's voice. The question was innocent enough, but it was laced with a dangerous undercurrent. "The sandwich is great," she answered him, realizing neither of them had spoken in a long time. Bad manners on her part. He was her client. She should be entertaining him. "I was just thinking about…about something. If you're done eating, why don't you flip through these brochures and see if any of the new styles catch your eye?"

As he unfolded one of the colorful brochures, Megan noticed his hands—tanned, long-fingered, solid but with a certain grace. She wondered what he did for a living. Dressed as he was, in khaki slacks and a teal blue polo shirt, he didn't appear to be in the work mode. Maybe today was his day off.

"Are you looking for something traditional, or do you want a more modern approach?"

"I don't know," he said gruffly. Haphazardly, it seemed, he pointed to one of the pictures. "This one." He had, instinctively perhaps, chosen the most expensive kitchen in the group, a sleekly modern look with white enamel cabinetry and green marble countertops. "How much would a kitchen like this cost?"

"You're looking at about fifty thousand dollars," she said without blinking.

Surprisingly, Holt didn't blink, either. "I don't think it would be wise to invest that much in my house. I would never get it back when I sell."

"Oh, so you're planning on selling?"

"No." He barked out the word.

"Well, don't worry," Megan continued, unperturbed. She'd dealt with difficult clients before. "I can achieve a look similar to this green-and-white model at less than half the cost. That's one thing I'm really good at—budget re-modeling that looks like you spent a whole lot more. Depending on the size of your kitchen, the price may drop even further."

"It's a big kitchen," he told her. "I have one of those old houses in Lakewood."

"Excellent! I've always loved those big old homes. Has the kitchen ever been updated?"

"Not since the 1940s."

"Then you really do need a change. When can I come over and see it?"

"Come over?" Odd, but Megan thought she saw a flash of panic in his smoky eyes.

"That's the place to start," she said. "I have to take measurements. Then I can do some drawings and crunch numbers. Do you have a budget in mind?"

"Something under fifty thousand dollars would be nice," he said dryly.

She smiled. "I understand. When would be a convenient time for me to see the kitchen?"

Again, he seemed uncomfortable at the prospect of her visiting his home. She wondered why. Was it such a disaster that he was embarrassed?

"Wednesday," he finally answered, as if it were a royal edict. "Day after tomorrow. One o'clock."

She would have to juggle some other appointments, but she wasn't about to debate. She had this odd feeling that he was on the verge of walking away without a backward glance, and she didn't want him to do that. Big contracts in Lakewood were too hard to come by. She could use the commission and the prestige this job could bring to her.

He provided her with an address, but not a home phone number. "If you need to cancel or something, call me at work," he said, handing her a business card.

Ram Nurseries. "Oh, I know this place. I bought tulip bulbs there last spring, to plant in the beds on my patio, but... now that I think about it, they didn't come up."

"You probably didn't refrigerate them long enough."

"Refrigerate them? Why would I do that?"

"The Texas climate is too warm for tulips," he replied, as if stating the obvious. "You have to fool them into thinking they've been wintering up north before they'll bloom."

"No kidding? Learn something new every day." She gathered the brochures into a neat stack. "You can take these home. I imagine your wife might have something to say about the new kitchen." Megan held her breath. She had to know for sure.

Holt's face became so still, he could have been carved from marble. "Shelley always did want a big, shiny new kitchen with all the latest appliances. We bought the house with the intention of remodeling, but then... well, it never seemed to get done."

"It's high time, then," Megan said, stifling a totally irrational disappointment. She should have known a good-looking, successful businessman like Holt Ramsey would be taken. Not that *she* wanted him. Even if he did make her blood race through her veins, he wasn't exactly a warm person. He reminded her of a tiger she'd once seen at the circus—civilized on the outside, but just give him an excuse and he would lash out.

Anyway, she had enough trouble convincing her colleagues she was for real without ruining her reputation by making a play for a client. She forced a smile. "I'm sure Mrs. Ramsey will be delighted that you've taken the first step."

Holt slid out of the booth and stood, treating her to a penetrating stare. "I didn't mean to mislead you. Shelley, my wife, died two years ago. For a long time, I couldn't bear the thought of carrying through with any of the plans we'd made together. But you're right, it's high time. I'll see you on Wednesday."

Megan stared after him as he strode swiftly toward the door, wanting to kick herself for bringing up the subject of wives. She shouldn't have been so curious. How ghastly for a man to lose a young wife. She wondered if Holt had any kids.

She hoped he didn't plan to install an expensive designer kitchen as a tribute to the late Shelley. Megan didn't think she could handle the emotions that would surround such a project. Only recently had she pulled her psyche together and turned her own life around, putting behind her the grieving, the guilt and the low self-esteem. Despite the brave, brash face she showed to the world, she was too fragile to take on anyone else's ravaged feelings.

Holt climbed into his Porsche, cursing the late summer heat, cursing his big mouth. Megan was the one who'd brought up the subject of his wife, but he was the one who'd let that melodramatic speech about Shelley spew forth. He was done grieving for Shelley. He had loved her from the time they were kids, and it was tragically unfair that she'd been taken from him so young, but that was two years ago. It was time for things to return to normal.

His hormones, certainly, were back in shape, if his reaction to Megan Carlisle was any indication. He had wanted to dislike her—had *tried* to dislike her. The woman had abandoned her child because she couldn't be bothered. It wasn't as if she hadn't been able to afford to raise the child. She had put him up for adoption, then blithely continued her high-society life in a whirlwind of parties, Ivy League schools and the Junior League. But after spending only a few minutes with her, he would swear she didn't have a selfish or malicious bone in her body. In fact, she seemed as sweet and ingenuous as a puppy, but a whole lot sexier. Damn, she did things to him.

Don't even think *about it,* he warned himself sternly. To follow up on those inner rustlings of desire was out of the question. His sole purpose was to make sure the woman would be a positive influence on Brian, and then allow them to meet. Beyond that, there would be nothing. He didn't believe for a minute, no matter how sweet Megan was on the surface, that she would consider any sort of long-term relationship with her son.

As he entered his sprawling stone house, he smelled smoke. "Brian?" he called out sharply.

"In the kitchen, Dad. I burned something."

Relieved that the house wasn't about to go up in flames, Holt made his way to the kitchen, where his gangly fourteen-year-old son was struggling with a casserole dish at the sink, trying to scrape a layer of blackened goo from the inside.

"I tried to make macaroni and cheese—you know, in the oven, the way Mom used to. But I screwed it up."

"So it appears. I'm surprised the smoke alarm didn't go off."

"It did. I had to take the batteries out."

"Let the pan soak awhile," Holt suggested.

"That's what I wanted to do. But you always yell when I leave dishes in the sink."

"I'll make an exception this time. You know, I really wish you wouldn't try to cook when I'm not home." Holt seldom worried about leaving Brian alone. He'd been a latchkey kid since he was ten, and he was unusually responsible for a boy his age. But Holt still liked to make the appropriate worried-parent sounds from time to time.

"Are you telling me you could have helped?" Brian asked, one eyebrow raised in disbelief.

"Well, no, I guess not. But I could have helped you put out the fire, if there'd been one."

Holt looked around him at the cavernous old kitchen with new eyes. It really was shabby. Cheap, crookedly hung wooden cabinets sported uncounted layers of paint, the most recent a pinkish beige. The ancient countertops had more hills and valleys than a golf course, and the single-well sink, stained and pitted, was hopelessly outdated. The refrigerator was slightly more modern—1970s avocado green. The old gas stove, circa 1945, worked sporadically, and though Holt had had it inspected, he still sometimes feared it would leak and blow up the whole house. The uneven floor was covered with cracked and peeling gray linoleum. The only concessions to modern life were a microwave, which prepared virtually all of his and Brian's meals, and a coffeemaker.

Yeah, it was high time. He turned to Brian. "You want me to fix you some lunch?"

"That's okay," he said dejectedly. "I can nuke a TV dinner as easy as you can."

Poor Brian. Holt knew his son missed his mother's excellent Southern cooking. So did Holt. Maybe a new kitchen would inspire them both to learn how to cook.

"Dad," Brian said after he'd thrown a Salisbury steak into the microwave, "have you made any progress? You know, with finding my real mom?"

Holt bristled. "Mom was your real mom. Parenthood has a lot more to do with raising a child than do genes and chromo—"

"You know what I mean. My birth mother, then."

Holt unruffled his feathers. He understood why it was suddenly so important for Brian to find his roots. He missed his mother terribly, and he was hoping, on some deep, subconscious level, perhaps, to find a substitute.

"You know," Holt said, "I'm afraid you'll be disappointed. Do you have any idea who your biological mother is likely to be?"

Brian's expression grew serious. "I'm not a dope, Dad. She was probably an unwed teenager, and she didn't want me. But I hope…well, I'd like to think she had a hard time giving me up, and I want to let her know that I don't hold it against her. I understand, I really do. There's a girl in my class, Ruthie Dell, who's pregnant, and she's gonna give her baby up for adoption so it can have a better life. I wouldn't mind if my mother was someone like Ruthie."

"She might not want to meet you," Holt cautioned.

"I know. But I still want to find out. I don't think Mom would mind."

No, Shelley wouldn't have begrudged her adopted son's curiosity. Brian meant no disrespect at all. "There has been some progress made," Holt said carefully. "The private investigator hopes to locate your natural mother soon, but he hasn't made any promises."

Brian smiled excitedly. "Way to go."

Holt smiled back. This was the most animated he'd seen his son since Shelley had died. God, he loved that kid. He would die before he would let anyone hurt Brian again.

Two

When she completed her afternoon appointments, Megan returned to her office and shut the door, only then allowing herself the luxury of again thinking about her new client.

Holt Ramsey. The name matched the man—strong, hard, no-nonsense. She should have been excited about the possibility of remodeling his kitchen. If it was as big and old as he'd led her to believe, and if he had a reasonable budget, she could make his kitchen a showplace, the crown jewel in her portfolio.

But she wasn't as excited about the work as she was intrigued with the man himself. Of course, nothing would happen. Nothing *could* happen, she wouldn't let it. But his mere proximity made her whole body jump to awareness.

She looked around her office and wrinkled her nose in disgust. The place was a sty. Ordinarily, she didn't worry about the mess, because she usually met her clients on their turf. But Holt Ramsey must have been appalled to find that the ace kitchen designer he'd been expecting was in reality a slob. There was just so much work to do and so little time to keep things organized. Sometime soon she would have to take off a weekend and shovel out the place.

She spied the pile of pink message slips and remembered the call from Heather. Did she dare return it? She had pushed that part of her life far behind her, and the prospect of dredging up any portion of it frightened her a little.

But why had Heather called? There must be a reason. Figuring curiosity would get to her sooner or later, she reached for the wrinkled pink paper.

"Hello?" a pleasant voice answered. Megan could hear a child crying in the background.

"Heather?"

"Megan? Oh my God, Megan, it's you, isn't it?"

"Yes. Yes, it's me. H-how are you?" Odd how difficult those three words were to speak, Megan thought. She and Heather used to spend hours on the phone with never a quiet moment between them.

"I'm just fine, just— Oh, Megan, I know you probably don't want to talk to me and I understand, but I have a real reason for calling. Someone's trying to track you down. A private investigator came nosing around here. He's questioning your old classmates, looking for you."

"Why?" Megan's heart hammered erratically behind her ribs.

"He wouldn't say. I didn't tell him where you were."

Dozens of questions whirled through her mind. "Why did you...I mean, who would...am I that hard to find?"

"Apparently so. You're not in the phone book. I called your mother to get your number, but she probably wouldn't have given it to a stranger."

Megan was surprised her mother still *had* her number, as little as she'd used it over the past few years.

"The weird thing is, this private detective was asking about Daniel, too."

Suddenly it seemed as if all the oxygen had been sucked out of the room. *Daniel?* Why? "Wouldn't we all like to know where Daniel is."

"I didn't tell this guy anything, Megan. But I thought...well, I have his number, if you'd like to call him yourself. I don't know about you, but if someone were looking for me, I'd want to know who and why."

"Yes, I'd like the number." She wrote down the information on the back of the original message slip and stuck it to her filing cabinet with a magnet. "Heather—"

"Megan—" Heather said at the same time. They both paused awkwardly. Heather forged ahead. "I never got the chance to tell you before how sorry I was—"

"I never gave you the chance," Megan countered.

"Nevertheless, I want to tell you now. It was so awful, your losing the baby and Daniel disappearing all at the same time. I don't know how you managed."

"Badly," Megan said with a shaky laugh.

"But it's better now, right? I've always tried to believe things turned out okay for you."

"Things aren't bad." And that was the truth, she realized with a start. Her mother wasn't speaking to her, her father had cut her out of his will on his deathbed, but still she'd managed to find some measure of satisfaction in her newfound career.

"I'm glad." The crying in the background increased in volume. "Listen, I have to go. Call me sometime. Maybe we can go to lunch." Heather said it like she didn't believe it would ever happen.

"I will," Megan replied, fully intending to follow up. She hadn't realized until this moment what a disservice she'd done to herself by losing touch with Heather.

After hanging up, Megan had to swallow back unwelcome tears. She'd been out of her mind with grief when, after her baby was taken from her, she'd returned to Dallas and found no trace of Daniel. He and his father had moved, left town without a forwarding address. She should have turned to Heather for comfort. But instead she'd folded inward, unwilling to share her feelings with anyone.

Pulling herself together, she dialed the private investigator's number. As she waited for him to be paged, she thought again of Holt Ramsey. Did he have something to do with this odd development? His sudden appearance was awfully mysterious, come to think of it. He claimed to have been referred by an anonymous voice at a party, and that sounded fishy. He'd also been rather vague about his kitchen remodeling plans, as if he hadn't given it much thought—and possibly didn't intend to.

The P.I. answered the phone with a grunt.

"This is Megan Carlisle," she said crisply. "I understand you've been looking for me. Mind telling me why?"

There was a long pause. "I don't know why. I was hired to find you. I did. I've been paid, and I'm out of it. Satisfied?"

"Who hired you?"

"Can't tell you. Client confidentiality, ya know." He hung up before she could interrogate him further.

Megan set the receiver in its cradle and slumped into her chair. Who was looking for her, and why? Other than getting pregnant as a teenager and being shuffled off to a small town in Oklahoma to have the baby, her life was an open book. Not a pretty picture book, perhaps, but open nonetheless. No one from her past would have to resort to investigators to find her. Her mother, although she wasn't currently speaking to Megan, knew exactly where to find her. So did her ex.

It probably came down to money, she decided. Her father, Cramer Carlisle, had been a millionaire twenty times over when he'd died. Perhaps someone had jumped to the wrong conclusion that Megan had inherited a chunk of the family fortune, and they planned to swindle her or something.

That was a joke. Her father had disinherited her, and her mother would leave the estate to her cats before she would give Megan a penny. And all because Megan had committed the unpardonable sin of divorcing the philandering, mean-tempered husband they had chosen for her.

If Holt Ramsey had anything to do with these strange goings-on, she was determined she would find out on Wednesday.

Holt cursed his luck. Of all days for Brian to come down with a bad cold, did it have to be today, when Megan was coming over? Holt had been counting on Brian to be safely away from the house all day at soccer camp.

Holt had tried to get hold of Megan and cancel the appointment, but her office hadn't been able to reach her. Fortunately, Brian was upstairs in bed, dozing on cold medicine and unlikely to venture downstairs. He had the TV and a stack of video games to keep him occupied should he wake up.

The doorbell rang at precisely one o'clock. Steeling himself for his inevitable reaction to her, Holt opened the door. She was like a fresh spring breeze on that parched August day, dressed in a slim white skirt and brightly flowered cotton jacket. Her long hair was tied back loosely with a pink scarf. She carried her ubiquitous armload of sample books and other paraphernalia, including a chain of laminate color samples that dangled from her wrist like a bracelet. He wondered if she ever went anywhere without being loaded down like a pack mule.

"Hi!" she greeted him brightly as she looked around. "What a great house." Her sweeping gaze took in the high-ceilinged entry foyer with its outdated wallpaper, and the curving staircase with its heavily carved banister in desperate need of refinishing.

"Mmm-hmm," he murmured in reply, feeling strangely uncomfortable. Maybe it was because Megan was the first person since Shelley to see beyond the cosmetic nightmare his house represented. When Shelley had died, the plans for improvements had died with her. He wasn't sure he was ready to revive them. "Kitchen's this way."

"This chandelier is gorgeous," Megan said as they passed through the formal living room, her head swiveling from side to side as she took it all in. "You know, with a few renovations, this place could be a palace. NuWorld just does kitchens, but I wouldn't mind giving you a hand with the rest of the house, when you're ready."

He glanced over his shoulder at her. "You moonlight on the side, then?" he asked suspiciously, almost hoping to discover some unattractive, opportunistic streak in her.

She shook her head. "Oh, no. I'd do it for free. I look at the place the way an artist views a blank canvas, you know? Besides, maybe I'll get some referrals from it."

He held open the swinging door into the kitchen, making no reply to her offer. If he did any further renovations, he wouldn't have Megan Carlisle in the middle of things. He wouldn't give her any excuses for hanging around. If and when he decided to introduce Brian and Megan, they would see each other on his terms.

As soon as she saw the kitchen, she gasped. Holt thought at first that she was horrified, but when he looked at her animated face, he realized the sheer awfulness of the place delighted her. "Oh, Mr. Ramsey, you didn't come to see me a moment too soon. This is..." Words escaped her.

"A nightmare?" he supplied.

"No! It has so much potential. Those big windows are fabulous. And the ceilings are so high. We can do a lot with storage. After I'm done, three professional chefs will be able to work in here without bumping into one another. Do you do a lot of cooking? Or do you have someone who comes in?"

"Neither."

She gave him a look that was downright suspicious. He supposed he wasn't acting like a typical client. "Are you really serious about this?" she asked sharply. "If you're not, please tell me now."

"I'm serious," he assured her. And maybe he was. He had become so indifferent to his surroundings that he'd forgotten how truly ugly the kitchen was.

Her easy smile returned. "Let's get started, then." She produced an industrial-size tape measure, some graph paper and a calculator. While he held the end of the tape, she efficiently measured, making various notes and calculations. Holt was acutely aware of her every move—the way her silk blouse molded to her breasts when she reached up high, the appealing swell of her slender hips when she leaned over. And those legs. How could such a petite woman have such long legs? The light from the windows played over those trim, firm calves as she stooped here and leaned there, driving his imagination wild.

When she was finished measuring, she sat down to produce a neat, precise floor plan. He sat across from her at the kitchen table, a scarred, cherrywood drop leaf that had belonged to both Holt's mother and his grandmother. He vividly remembered doing his homework sitting at this table.

Megan would probably want to get rid of it. It wouldn't fit in with the sleek new design.

"There's a folder around here somewhere with your name on it," Megan said, riffling through her stack. "Ah, here. I have included several samples and brochures for cabinets, countertops, wall coverings, appliances and floors. Why don't you glance through those and start narrowing down your choices while I finish up my sketches?"

As he perused the brochures, he took back everything he'd thought about her being incompetent. Obviously she knew exactly what she was doing. "Where did you learn how to do this?" he asked, curious despite himself.

"Went to school." She tapped out some numbers on the calculator. "I have a degree in interior design, but I have to confess I've learned more on the job at NuWorld than I ever did at school. I'm really lucky that Mr. Nelson, the owner, gave me a chance as green as I was. I'm still trying to prove myself. Mostly I've been given the unimportant, low-budget jobs no one else wants. But this job..." She positively glowed when she looked up at him. "I'll really show 'em."

Holt gulped. She was making it harder and harder for him to back out of having the remodeling done. "Is your position at NuWorld your first job, then?" he asked, playing the tough, demanding client.

"Yup. I know thirty-one is a little old to be entering the job market, but I got married during college, and my husband didn't want me to work. As soon as we split up, I went back to school to finish my degree. It took a long time. I had various part-time jobs then, to pay for school and all, but I don't count those."

Holt was flabbergasted. Her family had millions—oil money. Although her father had died several years ago, her mother was still sitting pretty, if her frequent appearances on the society pages were any indication. Why would Megan have to work her way through school? It was on the tip of his tongue to ask her, but of course, he couldn't. How would he explain his too-intimate knowledge of her family situation, which the P.I. had provided?

With every word she spoke, Megan Carlisle seemed less and less the self-absorbed woman he'd thought she would be.

"I still need to measure the height on those cabinets," she said. "I don't suppose you have a ladder, do you?"

"In the garage. I'll get it."

Megan hummed as she put the finishing touches on the floor plan. This was so much fun. She couldn't wait to get back to the office and work on the computer.

An insistent call roused her from her musings. "Dad? Hey, Dad!"

So, Mr. Ramsey did have children. The hoarse voice sounded so urgent that Megan felt compelled to locate it. It seemed to come from the servants' staircase off the kitchen. She followed the increasingly impatient summons up the stairs, arriving at a long hallway lined with many doors. Only one was open, and she went to it.

Inside the bedroom she found an adolescent boy lying in bed, his nose as red as Rudolph the Reindeer's. The floor was littered with wadded tissues, testament to a bad cold. He was cute, she thought. Not only that, but something about his looks struck a cord of familiarity. She couldn't put her finger on it, though.

He stared at her with wide hazel eyes, obviously startled. "Who are you?"

"I'm the kitchen designer," she said, giving what she hoped was a reassuring smile as she stepped into the room. "I'm here to look at your kitchen so I can work up a plan for a new design."

"Oh. Where's Dad?"

"In the garage, looking for a ladder. Is there something you needed?"

"I'm hungry. Dad said he would get me some stuff at Taco Mio for lunch."

"Mexican food? When you're sick?"

"It's just a cold. Anyway, there's not much choice. Dad's a lousy cook."

"What would you rather have, assuming someone would cook for you?" she asked impulsively.

"Uh... I don't know."

"How about chicken soup and a grilled-cheese sandwich? That's what my nanny used to make for me when I was sick."

The boy's eyes widened with brief anticipation before he slumped back on his pillow, dejected. "Real food, in this house? You know, it's cruel to get a sick person's hopes up."

She laughed. What a cute kid. All long limbs and angles and a nose too big for his face, but in a few years he would be a heartbreaker. Kind of like... yeah, that was it. He looked a bit like his father. "I'll see what I can do about lunch," she said before leaving him to his video games.

She'd seen the items she needed earlier, when she'd inspected the kitchen—a dusty can of chicken noodle soup in the back of the pantry, a wedge of cheddar cheese, two heels of bread and some butter in the almost-bare refrigerator. Five minutes later the soup was simmering and a grilled-cheese sandwich was browning in the pan on the stove. Judging from the state of the Ramseys' cookware, no one had touched a pot or pan around here in years. Megan was glad she could provide the kid—she'd forgotten to ask his name—with one home-cooked meal, simple though it was.

"What the hell are you doing?"

The angry voice scared her half to death. She whirled around to find Holt, cobwebs clinging to his hair, a smudge on his cheek and a scrape on his right forearm. He was holding a ladder and staring at her as if she'd just committed a mortal sin.

"I'm fixing lunch for your son."

"My—" The ladder slipped out of his grasp and clattered to the floor. "Did you see him?" he demanded, grabbing Megan's upper arms in a painful grip. "Did you meet him?"

"Yes, I met him, and would you let go of me, please?"

Holt relaxed his grasp, but he didn't release her. "Who said you could go upstairs?"

"Well, excuse me, but I couldn't ignore a child crying out for help. Your son was calling rather persistently for you and, since you were busy in the garage, I went upstairs to see what the problem was. Turns out he was just hungry. Really, how could you even consider giving a sick child that greasy food from Taco Mio? And if you don't let go of me, I'm going to kick you where it counts."

Finally he let her go. At least he had the good grace to look penitent. "Sorry. I guess I just, um..."

Megan turned her back on him, worried that he might see more in her face that she wanted him to. When he'd held on to her, she should have been frightened. Instead she'd felt...excited. There was a lot of passion inside that man. She shivered at the thought of seeing that passion guided into other channels.

She flipped the sandwich and stirred the soup as casually as she dared. "What is your problem?"

He released a pent-up breath. "There's no problem, really. I overreacted. Brian is sick and I don't want you to catch his bug. You might sue me or something."

Megan found that the most pitiful excuse for an explanation she'd ever heard. Figuring she had nothing to lose, she asked, "What do you know about a private investigator named Benny Powell who's been nosing around in my life?''

She watched Holt from the corner of her eye, but his features were now rigidly schooled. "Never heard of him."

Megan considered his answer. He might be telling the truth. She flipped the sandwich onto a plate, then turned both burners off. "Mr. Ramsey, I'd like to do your kitchen, I really would. But there's been something funny about this job all along, and I don't think I can handle it. Whether you're playing games with me or—or you want to build a kitchen as a tribute to your wife, I don't think I'll stick around. You make me very uncomfortable."

With that she set down the spatula, returned to the kitchen table and began gathering up her things. She hated herself for giving up. The commission on this kitchen would have given her bank account a welcome boost, and the prestige of such a job would do wonders for her image at NuWorld. But Holt Ramsey was an unknown quantity who frankly scared her a bit, never mind that he was the sexiest male to cross her path in ages.

With mixed feelings, Holt watched Megan pack up her things. Part of him wanted to stop her, to apologize for behaving like a jackass. But a wiser part of him prevailed. He'd been nuts to allow her inside his house when Brian was home. What if she had recognized him? Although Brian didn't resemble Megan herself, he could be the spitting image of his father, or someone in Megan's family. As suspicious as Megan was of his motives, she might have put it together.

Of course, that was the point, wasn't it? To allow Brian and Megan to meet?

Maybe not. Megan Carlisle was a little on the flighty side. How could Holt be sure she would take a responsible attitude toward her relationship with Brian? He wouldn't allow her to flit in and out of their lives, raising Brian's hopes and then dashing them to bits.

"You'd better take that sandwich and soup up to Brian before they get cold," she said. "I can find my way out." She disappeared from view the same way she'd come in, on the tail of a breeze. Her perfume, a young, playful fragrance, lingered in the air for a few seconds, and then it, too, was gone.

Shaking his head, Holt poured some of the soup into a bowl, put it and the sandwich onto a tray, added a glass of milk and headed up the back stairs.

Brian's eyes lit up with delight when he saw the tray. "A grilled cheese and chicken soup? Wow, she did it. She actually did it. I didn't think it was possible. Dad, you didn't tell me you were gonna redo the kitchen."

"I'm not," he said as he set the tray over Brian's blanket-covered legs. "Ms. Carlisle wanted to give me a bid, but I'm sure it'll be too expensive."

"Get real, Dad. We both know you have enough money stashed in the bank for ten kitchens." He slurped up several spoonfuls of soup. "Even if your business wasn't doing good, there's Mom's insurance money."

"That money's for you," Holt said, tightly clipping off the words.

"C'mon, how many college educations do you think you'll need to finance?" A quarter of the sandwich disappeared into Brian's mouth. "Let's get a new kitchen. Man, this lunch is great." He noisily spooned more of the soup into his mouth.

"For Pete's sake, it's just a grilled cheese and canned soup."

"Yeah. A step up from what we've *been* eating. When that lady came to the bedroom door, I thought I was dreaming or something. Man, she was pretty. Va-va-voom."

"Brian!" Oh, God, Holt thought.

"What? I got hormones. It's not disrespectful to say a lady's pretty. Anyway, I mean she's pretty for you, not me. Why don't you take her out on a date? Maybe she'd cook a real dinner for us."

"I can't date a woman just so she can cook for us." Holt ran nervous fingers through his hair. This conversation had gotten entirely out of hand.

"So, forget the date and just ask her to come over and cook. I bet she would. She was awful nice."

That stopped him. "You really think so?"

"Yeah. Is there any more soup?"

"I'll get you a refill. If I'd known you liked soup, I'd have made you some before now."

"You'd have probably burned it," Brian said under his breath.

"You got a smart mouth," Holt shot back, but he tempered the scolding with a smile. He started to leave the room, tray in hand, then paused. "I'll see what Ms. Carlisle has to say about the kitchen."

As he warmed up the soup in the microwave, Holt mulled over his choices. Obviously Brian and Megan had hit it off. Brian would never forgive him if he knew Holt had scared off his birth mother. Holt couldn't dismiss Megan from their lives, not yet. Somehow he would have to convince her that he really wanted his kitchen remodeled, and that she was the one to do it.

Three

Megan saw the dark green Porsche the minute she turned into NuWorld's parking lot. She knew of only one person who drove that kind of car, and that didn't bode well for her Friday morning. So much for her plan to slip into an untroubled weekend. Holt Ramsey exemplified trouble.

She pulled her battered Jeep next to his pristine sports car, surprised to find the man himself sitting behind the steering wheel—waiting for her, apparently. The realization gave her a case of nerves, causing her to clumsily upend her purse, dumping half the contents onto the passenger seat floorboard.

"For pity's sake," she muttered as she scooped up her things. For once she would like to meet the man when she didn't have a big mess on her hands. But as usual she had brought work home with her, and her car looked like a national disaster area.

Having postponed the inevitable for as long as possible, she opened her door and put on a pleasant but distant face. Above all, she had to remain professional. If Mr. Nelson discovered she'd turned down a job the size of Holt Ramsey's kitchen, she might well find herself unemployed.

"Good morning," Holt greeted her, offering a polite hand to assist her out of the Jeep. She noticed that he was careful not to touch her until she nodded, giving him permission. Then he guided her down to the pavement with a gentle hand at her elbow. His demeanor was quite a switch from the impersonal, almost rude man she'd seen two days ago.

She'd hoped that his nearness wouldn't affect her as it had the other day. Her hopes were in vain. "Thank you," she murmured, marveling at the warmth of his touch, and how every nerve ending in her hand seemed to tingle with life. "I assume my finding you here isn't a coincidence."

"No, I was waiting for you." His unexpected smile sparkled with mischief and no small amount of charm. "Do you have time for a cup of coffee?"

She glanced at her watch, stalling. She had plenty of time, but did she really want to spend it with him? She felt like a coiled spring around him. She hadn't been lying when she'd told him he made her uncomfortable, but it was an exciting sort of uncomfortable, like sitting at a movie thriller, waiting for the inevitable explosion of gunshots or the bad guy jumping out of the closet.

"Okay," she finally said, her curiosity winning out over common sense, "a quick cup of coffee." She left everything but her purse in her vehicle, feeling pleasantly unencumbered for a change as they walked to the same deli around the corner where they'd had lunch earlier in the week.

The place was crowded. When Megan saw a couple vacating a small table by the window she grabbed it while Holt got their coffee. He joined her a few minutes later, but apparently he was in no hurry to make his purpose known to her. He stared out the window and said nothing as the seconds ticked away.

She didn't push him, hoping that in his own time he would tell her what the heck was going on. She sipped leisurely at her amaretto coffee and studied him without pretense, enjoying what she saw. He was one finely sculpted hunk of virility—she would give him that.

"I didn't mean to scare you away the other day," he finally said. "I'm very overprotective of my son. He went through a terrible time when his mother died...."

"But why would you have to protect him from me? What possible threat was I?"

"I can't explain it. I behaved irrationally. I can assure you it won't happen again. I want you to do the kitchen."

"If you really want the work done, I can refer you to another designer at NuWorld. Sheena Berenson is the top—"

"No, I want you to do it."

"Why? I've already told you I'm the most junior designer on staff, and I don't have much experience with big-budget jobs. Now, Sheena—"

"I like the way you work."

Again, Megan could feel undercurrents. There was something Holt wasn't telling her. She longed to simply tell him no. But the specter of unemployment again raised its ugly head. She sighed, realizing that for the sake of her career she would have to do his damned kitchen. "All right," she said.

"Thank you. You won't regret it." He smiled then, setting her heart to fluttering like a frantic, caged bird. "My son was pretty mad that I chased you off. He was most impressed with you. He raved about your soup and sandwich.''

''It was just canned soup and a grilled cheese.''

''Around our house, that's something like a miracle.''

''My word, how do you survive? What do you live on?'' Megan loved to cook. She couldn't imagine anyone not knowing how to fix something as basic as a grilled cheese.

''TV dinners and fast food,'' Holt admitted. ''Now don't give me that look. Some of it's pretty nutritious.''

She shrugged. ''It's not my place to judge how you eat.'' But she couldn't stop thinking about that boy, and how his eyes had lit up at the prospect of home cooking. When she spoke again, it was for the boy's sake—not the father's. ''Tell you what. Why don't I come over some night and fix you two a *real* home-cooked meal? That way I could get a feel for your kitchen, figure out how the work flows. It would help me do a more efficient design.''

Holt's eyebrows flew up. ''Do you normally get that involved with your remodeling jobs?''

''Frankly, no. But this *is* an important job, and I want you to be completely satisfied. Besides, every once in a while your kid deserves to eat something that doesn't come out of a bag or a box.''

Her accusation produced a brief look of guilt on Holt's handsome face, and Megan wondered if she'd gone too far. What Brian Ramsey ate was really none of her business.

The expression passed quickly. ''All right, you're on. I'll even buy the groceries, if you'll give me a list. How about Saturday? Seven o'clock?''

''Fine. I'll make out the list right now.'' She knew the ingredients for lasagna by heart. She fished in her purse for pen and paper.

''This isn't a date,'' Holt said, his newfound charm abruptly fleeing.

She didn't look up from her list. "Certainly not."

"Just so you're clear on that. Nothing personal, but I don't date."

She peeked up at him through her lashes, and a poignant sadness washed over her, way out of proportion to the situation. Why did she care? So what if his face looked as bleak as a desert? It wasn't her job to help him work through his grief for his wife.

As she continued the list, she tried to ignore her growing sense of foreboding. This situation was more than a little weird. But she was so drawn to him, as much by curiosity as pure physical magnetism, that she couldn't make herself back out of the deal she'd struck.

Finally she handed him the piece of paper. "I'll bring over some preliminary sketches, too," she said. "But just so *you're* clear—I reserve the right to turn the job over to Sheena if I find out things aren't what you say they are."

Her ultimatum gave him pause. "I suppose that's only fair," he finally said, cementing in Megan's mind the fact that he *did* have some hidden agenda.

Her mind conjured up several unsavory possibilities, all of which she quickly dismissed. He couldn't possibly be a serial killer or rapist, and he was too established in Dallas to be a con artist—his nurseries had been around for years. No, there was something much more subtle motivating Holt Ramsey's sudden interest in her. She simply had to find out what it was.

Holt was trimming the junipers in the front yard, something he'd neglected for weeks, when Brian bounced out the door, obviously over the worst of his cold.

"The coach called," he announced. "He said there's room in next week's soccer camp, so I can make up the days I missed. Hey, how come you're suddenly so interested in how the house looks? I heard you vacuuming this morning, and the downstairs bathroom smells clean.''

"We've lived like derelict bachelors long enough," Holt declared. "It's time we fixed up this house like we planned. It's pretty embarrassing when a professional landscape architect has the ugliest yard on the block."

An unabashed grin brightened Brian's face. "Cool. Does this have anything to do with Ms. Carlisle?"

Darn kid was too smart for his own good. "Sort of," Holt hedged. "She's coming over to make dinner tonight." He threw this out casually.

Brian was shocked. "You mean you actually asked her to fix us dinner? Dad, I was only kidding. How totally rude!"

"Hey, it was all her idea. She wants to check out how the kitchen works and, at the same time, treat a couple of domestically impaired males to a home-cooked meal. How could I say no?"

"I guess I wouldn't have, either. But, man, it seems kinda cold, you know? What does she get out of the deal?"

A chance to know her son. With a flash of insight, Holt realized he had to tell Brian about Megan. He had no right to manipulate these two people, one of whom he loved very much. The longer he postponed it, the angrier they both would be when he told them the truth. And he really didn't have much choice but to tell them, especially when he couldn't come up with one truly negative thing about Megan.

He wiped a trickle of perspiration from his brow. "It's hot out here," he said abruptly. "Let's go in and make some lemonade, and I'll tell you something about Ms. Carlisle."

Brian followed Holt inside, eyeing him curiously as he pulled a can of lemonade concentrate from the freezer and stuck it under the hot water tap to thaw.

"The pitcher's in the dishwasher," Brian offered. "Want me to wash it?"

"You'll be amazed to know I ran a load of dishes this morning. The pitcher—" he opened the dishwasher with a flourish "—is clean."

"Cool. What did you want to tell me about Ms. Carlisle?"

Holt's hands shook as he opened the lemonade can. "I don't know how else to tell you this except to just blurt it out. Megan is your birth mother."

Several seconds of stunned silence followed Holt's abrupt announcement. Brian's mouth hung open and his eyes bulged. When he finally spoke, his eyes narrowed suspiciously and his words surprised Holt. "So, that's why she was so eager to fix me lunch, and now dinner. I guess she feels like she has a lot of mothering to make up for."

"No, no, that's not it," Holt said quickly, amazed at how ready he was to defend Megan. "Brian, she doesn't even know who you are. She was just being nice."

"She doesn't know... you mean you haven't told her?"

"Not yet. And I won't, if you don't want me to."

"That's not very fair to her. You brought her over here under false pretenses, pretending you wanted a new kitchen."

"I do want a new kitchen," Holt protested. "But you're right, I probably should have told her up front, as soon as I found her. It's just... I wanted to check her out first, you know?"

"You mean, if she'd turned out to be a drug addict or a prostitute or something, you wouldn't have ever told me you'd found her," Brian concluded.

Reluctantly, Holt nodded. "I just wanted to protect you."

Brian's sudden surge of temper was startling. "I don't *need* protecting!" he lashed out. "I thought you would've figured that out by now. Do you remember how mad I was after you finally told me Mom had cancer? That was only about a month before she died. I kept asking, and you kept saying everything was fine. When you finally told me the truth, I was madder than hell. I kept thinking about all that time we'd wasted." The anger seemed to trickle out of him. "I would have been with her more if I'd known she was dying. I'd have . . . I don't know, I'd have been a better kid, I guess."

"You were a—you *are* a great kid," Holt objected, shaken by Brian's passionate outburst. "And I had no idea you were mad at me." Brian had been silent and sullen after Shelley's death, but Holt had assumed that was just a natural state of grieving.

"Yeah, well, I got over it," Brian said quietly.

"I'm sorry," Holt said. "I thought you were too young to understand or handle your mom's illness, but I guess I was wrong. And I'm sorry I've bungled this whole thing about Megan, too." He paused before asking, "What should I do now?"

The fact that Holt had asked for guidance from his son seemed to quell Brian's anger. "We gotta tell her," he said without hesitation.

"All right. But I think it might be wise for me to tell her when you're not around—like after dinner."

"Yeah, she might freak, and she probably wouldn't want to do that in front of me," Brian said with a level of understanding that surprised his father.

Holt breathed a sigh of relief. So far, so good. Brian, usually an easygoing kid, had shown signs of a temper Holt had hardly been aware of. But the emotion was perfectly justified, and at least the boy's spurt of hostility had been short-lived. He could only hope Megan Carlisle would take the news as well.

* * *

Megan immediately noticed the carefully sculpted ever-
greens and freshly mown grass when she pulled up to the
curb in front of the Ramseys's house. The landscaping made
a world of difference to the old stone structure. Some trim
paint and a new awning to replace the faded tatters that
hung over the front windows would help even more.

Lord, what she wouldn't give for a free hand and a hundred or so thousand dollars to give this house a facelift! It
was a crime to let such potential go to waste. But then, the
house belonged to Holt, and he could do what he wanted.
A new kitchen was at least a step in the right direction.

She had brought her design ideas with her. Since this
wasn't a "date," there was no harm in mixing business with
pleasure. Given her nearly uncontrollable physical reaction
to the man, she figured it was a good idea to keep their relationship on firm professional footing, anyway. With her
mind safely occupied with all the myriad details a remodeling job of this magnitude entailed, she wouldn't have time
to dwell on silly fantasies.

She grabbed a stack of folders and headed for the front
door.

Brian answered. He stared at her, speechless, like she was
some new specimen of bug he'd caught in a jar.

"I'm Megan Carlisle, the kitchen designer—remember?"

He nodded mutely.

"I'm here to show you guys some new designs and, uh,
fix dinner. Oh, dear, I came on the right day, didn't I?"

"Yeah," he said, finally finding his voice. "C'mon in.
Dad's still getting dressed. He comes home from work all
sweaty."

Megan wasn't surprised. The temperature had risen above a hundred today, for the third straight day. "You look like you're feeling better."

"Yeah. Thanks for the soup and sandwich." He led her into the kitchen, where several plastic grocery sacks sat on the counter. "That's the stuff you asked for. You don't have to wait for Dad before you get started, do you?"

"Are you that hungry?"

"Starved."

"Okay." She rummaged through the sacks for tomato paste, fresh garlic and the other ingredients she needed for the sauce. Then she opened various drawers and cabinets until she rounded up all the cookware she needed. The kitchen was actually fairly well equipped. Shelley must have been a good cook.

As she worked, she felt Brian's steady, curious gaze on her. Heavens, was cooking so foreign to the Ramsey males that her preparations were a curiosity?

The sauce was simmering and the noodles boiling by the time Holt made an appearance. Megan heard the swinging door open. She felt his overwhelming presence even before she turned around and saw him.

"Sorry I'm running late," he said.

It was all she could do not to gape at him. The other times she'd seen him, he'd looked casually professional in a yuppie sort of way, in loose khakis and polo shirts. Tonight he was wearing blue jeans faded almost to white and a Dallas Cowboys T-shirt that was about a half size too small.

She got the impression that he had deliberately dressed down for her, as if to prove to her this really wasn't a date. But he couldn't have looked sexier if he'd tried. Those jeans clung to every line of muscle in his thighs, and the snug shirt only emphasized his broad shoulders and well-developed chest. Even his hair, which had been neatly combed on their other meetings, was ruffled, still damp from his shower and falling into natural waves, like he'd just toweled it dry and left it. *Or like a woman had just tousled it with her fingers.*

He walked over to the stove, lifted the lid on the sauce pot and inhaled. "Mmm, smells good."

Megan took an instinctive step back. His masculine appeal was so potent, she was afraid she would melt from it. Funny, but every time she saw him, her reaction grew stronger. She would never work up a healthy immunity to him at this rate.

"I've been watching her make it, Dad," Brian said. "It doesn't look *that* hard. Maybe I'll learn to cook."

"You do," Megan teased, "and the girls will be standing in line. A guy who cooks is infinitely interesting to women."

"I guess that means I'm a dead bore," Holt said.

He was anything but. However, she wouldn't tell *him* that. On this strictly undatelike evening, she would be careful not to say anything that could be misconstrued as flirting. Let him think she was as uninterested in his manly wiles as he appeared to be in her feminine ones.

"So, I guess you two are getting along okay, huh?" Holt asked with a brightness that rang false.

"Just fine," she replied.

"Uh, yeah," Brian said at the same time. Father and son exchanged a meaningful glance that perplexed Megan. Again she felt that undercurrent. Maybe they were testing her cooking skills. If she passed, they would hold her prisoner and make her cook every meal for them.

She stifled a chuckle. The oddest thing was, she didn't find the prospect all that unappealing. She just hoped that Holt would go ahead with the new kitchen. It would be a real pleasure to cook three meals a day in a beautiful, functional kitchen of her own design.

"I brought some sketches for you to look at," she said, nodding toward the folders she'd left on the cherrywood table. "Two of them are on the lines of what we discussed—clean, modern, with the white laminate cabinets. But I did another one just for fun, to see what you'd think. That cherrywood table would be beautiful if it were refinished, and it fits so nicely into that niche. So I designed the kitchen around it."

"Really?"

She tried to appear unconcerned as he studied the contents of the folder. Brian looked over his shoulder. The cherrywood design, which she'd done on impulse, had turned out to be her favorite, but it wasn't at all what Holt had asked for, so she was prepared for him to hate it.

"Is that really our kitchen?" Brian asked.

"I was about to ask the same thing," Holt said. "Could you really turn this ugly old cave into something that belongs in a magazine?"

"Absolutely," she answered with complete confidence, pleased that they seemed to like her work. She poured the pot of cooked lasagna noodles into a colander. "Do any of those designs work for you? Once I have something to start with, we can refine it."

"This one," Brian and Holt said together. She looked over, thrilled to see they were holding up the cherrywood kitchen.

"That's not at all like the one you chose the other day," she pointed out to Holt.

"But I didn't see anything like this the other day. Besides, I want to keep this table. It's an heirloom."

"No problem. Hey, this lasagna will take more than an hour. If y'all are really hungry, you can cube up this extra cheese and munch on it." She nodded toward a chunk of provolone, which sat on a cutting board.

Holt and Brian fell on the cheese like piranhas. Megan took that as a good sign. Their palates wouldn't be any too hard to please. She only hoped they weren't planning to hold up her culinary efforts to the sainted Shelley's.

Megan bit her lip, recognizing the unkind thought almost before it materialized. Was she actually jealous of a dead woman? She felt a familiar ache creeping around her heart and realized that, yes, she was a bit envious of the warm family life Shelley had no doubt enjoyed before she died—a handsome, hardworking husband, a healthy, normal child and a big old house on which to build dreams.

Of course, those dreams had been shattered, Megan reminded herself. She was alive and Shelley wasn't. It was downright awful of Megan to be unappreciative of the satisfying life she was building for herself, especially given her disastrous past. But sometimes she felt weighed down by the fact that she would probably never have a family of her own.

"You're awfully quiet over there." Holt's deep voice broke through her introspection. "Is everything going okay?"

"Mmm, fine." She looked down at the pan of layered noodles, sauce and cheeses, which she had assembled without any conscious effort. She was glad she'd chosen to cook a dish she could make in her sleep.

"Would the cook like some wine?" He thrust what appeared to be a glass of Chianti at her.

"Yes, I would. Thanks." Maybe the wine would relax her a bit. She was too keyed-up about what would probably turn into a pleasant but insignificant evening. She took a sip before setting the glass down so she could put the heavy lasagna pan into the oven. The old oven door shrieked in protest as Megan opened it, but the interior was plenty hot. She thrust the pan inside and shut the door.

As the dinner baked, filling the kitchen with a pleasant, spicy aroma, Megan put together a green salad, then melted butter and fresh garlic together for the garlic bread. The kitchen warmed up as did the conversation, aided by the wine, no doubt. But Megan never did feel completely comfortable. She had this persistent feeling that both Ramsey males were studying her, making some kind of judgment about her. She also couldn't deny that whatever the test was, she wanted to pass it.

Holt had to admit that he'd never enjoyed a meal more. Megan's lasagna tasted even better than it smelled. He helped himself to three servings, each with its own slice of garlic bread. Brian easily kept pace with him, and would have eaten more if Holt hadn't kicked him under the table. He didn't want Megan to think he'd been starving the kid.

The company wasn't bad, either. What had happened to all that good, healthy resentment he'd once harbored for the woman who had given away a wonderful kid like Brian?

At precisely eight forty-five, Brian looked at his watch and gave an elaborate yawn. "Well, it's been a long day. I think I'll turn in."

"At quarter 'til nine?" Holt said, his words laced with panic. As soon as Brian left him alone with Megan, he would have to tell her. He'd been hoping to have a few more sated, peaceful minutes to simply enjoy Megan's company.

"I've been sick, remember? Have to get my rest, you know." He gave Holt a meaningful stare and a nod before pushing himself from the table. "G'night, Ms. Carlisle. Thanks for dinner."

"Good night, Brian," she countered, looking bewildered. "I hope..." But she didn't get to finish her thought, whatever it was. Brian had beat a hasty retreat. "Does he always go to bed this early on a Saturday night?" she asked.

"Not usually. But when you were fourteen, how eager were you to spend the whole evening with adults?"

"Good point. Another five minutes, and we might have done something unforgivable, like draft him to do the dishes. Now I guess it's up to us." She stood and picked up her plate, then reached for his.

"Leave the dishes for now," Holt said. "I have something to discuss with you." He poured the last of the Chianti into their wineglasses. "Let's go out onto the patio. It should be cooling off by now."

Megan nodded, though her expression was wary, and followed him out the French doors to a flagstone terrace, where honeysuckle, trumpet vines and morning glory grew out of control around a gurgling fountain. It had always been one of Holt's favorite places, Shelley's, too. Toward the end, when she took pleasure in very little, she'd still enjoyed sitting out here and just listening to the running water, the birds, the insects.

The backyard was even more neglected than the front, Holt noted. Some aggressive pruning was in order.

"It's nice out here," Megan said, though she sat ramrod straight with her hand clenched around the stem of her glass, looking far from relaxed. She was a truly beautiful woman, Holt realized. Now, wearing a contemplative expression, she looked less like a pixie and more like an angel.

"Shelley and I weren't able to have children of our own," he began abruptly.

Megan's velvety brown eyes sharpened and focused on him, her interest apparent, but she said nothing.

"Brian is adopted," he continued. "Shelley's family attorney arranged for a private adoption. A friend of his had a teenage daughter who was unwed and pregnant." Holt watched Megan carefully, waiting for her to catch on. Bu she continued to simply look at him, her expression revealing little.

"We never met any of the other parties involved, never even knew their names," Holt said. "One day, the lawyer showed up with a four-day-old baby, and he was ours."

"That . . . that must have been a wonderful day for you," Megan said, her eyes unnaturally shiny.

Was that all the emotion she was going to show? Had she already known, perhaps, that Brian was her son? "You do know what I'm telling you, don't you?"

Her face went blank. "No."

Holt felt a crawly sensation at the back of his throat. What if she denied it, denied any responsibility for creating Brian? What would he tell the boy? Already Brian had pinned a lot of hopes on Megan. He liked her, Holt could tell that. And Megan seemed to like him.

"Holt, what is it?"

He supposed he was going to have to spell it out. "A few months ago, Brian became very curious about his biological parents. I don't really approve, mind you, but at the time it was the only thing he showed any interest in. So I hired a private investigator to look into the matter. The attorney who handled the adoption died several years ago, and all the records seem to have vanished, but the investigator still managed to track you down."

"Me? What do I have to do with this?"

Holt grew impatient with her innocent act. "I should think that would be apparent. You're Brian's natural mother."

Her mouth dropped open and she shook her head in denial. "I most certainly am not."

He'd been afraid of this. What was he going to tell Brian? He should just let her leave, get her out of their lives. But something pushed him, making him want to hurt her just as

Brian would be hurt at the knowledge that his mother wanted nothing to do with him. "Do you deny that when you were seventeen you gave birth to a child at the Good Shepherd Home in Eldon, Oklahoma?"

The wineglass slipped from her hands and shattered on the flagstones, sprinkling her bare legs with red droplets. "No, I don't deny it," she said, her chin tipped up belligerently. "But your private eye must be either grossly incompetent or grossly dishonest. I gave birth to a *girl,* Mr. Ramsey. Her name was Danielle Marie Carlisle, or it would have been if she hadn't been stillborn. And I can tell you this. If my baby had lived, I would never have given her up for adoption."

Holt was so shocked by Megan's impassioned speech that it was several seconds before he realized she had bolted out of her chair and was running away from him.

"Wait, Megan. Megan!" he called as he followed her through the French doors, which she'd left hanging open in her haste to escape. She was halfway to the front door before he caught her, swinging her around by her elbow. "Wait. We have to talk about this."

"No, we don't." Her lower lip trembled, almost undoing him. "Look, I don't appreciate this one bit. First you dig into my past, and then you drag me through this charade about remodeling your kitchen—"

"I was only trying to get to know you before I introduced you to Brian. The kid's been through a lot, and I didn't want another disappointment piled onto the ones he's already had."

"So, did I pass inspection?" she asked bitterly.

"With flying colors. Brian's crazy about you."

That softened her a bit. "I like him, too," she said. "And I'm sorry I'm not his mother, but I'm not. This is all some stupid mistake, and I suggest you stop payment on the check you wrote to Benny Powell until he straightens out the mess. Now, if you'll kindly let go of my arm, I'll be on my way."

Holt realized he'd been holding her in a tight, probably painful, grip. He released her immediately. The feel of her soft skin against his uncompromising hand lingered. "Are...are you sure it's a mistake?" he asked. "I have some pretty convincing evidence—"

"I don't care *what* you have. I did not give birth to Brian. I was there, remember?" she said before slipping out the front door.

He resisted the urge to follow her. Unless she was an awfully good liar, she was telling the truth—the truth as she knew it, anyway. Someone had made a mistake somewhere. But he wondered...was it Benny Powell's? He didn't think so. Benny's only error was that he didn't dig deep enough to discover the entire truth of Brian's parentage.

God, Holt felt terrible for having dredged up what was obviously a very painful memory for Megan. He had a feeling it might get worse before it got better.

You should stay the hell away from her, a voice inside his head whispered ominously. Hadn't he caused her enough distress?

Right now, he had a far more immediate concern. Brian was bounding down the stairs, scowling fiercely. "Aw, Dad, did you scare her away again?"

Four

Megan was still harboring a healthy dose of outrage on Monday morning as she sat in her office, trying to total a column of numbers. When she got yet a different answer on her third try, she pushed the calculator aside. Her train of thought was completely derailed.

She resented the hell out of what Holt Ramsey had done. He had manipulated her, lied to her and stirred up a host of memories she'd thought long buried.

She wanted to push all those dredged-up emotions aside as easily as she had the calculator, return them to the mental box where they'd been sleeping for years and nail down the lid. But it was too late. The memories were out, flying about her head like a flock of angry crows.

Cautiously she pulled herself back in time, probing the adolescent memories like a sore tooth to see how much she could endure. Her seventeenth year had started out a wonderful dream, but she'd ended it clutching at the shreds of a nightmare. She had loved Daniel Turner with all the intensity a seventeen-year-old could muster. The tough-talking, motorcycle-riding Daniel had been the bane of her strict, overprotective parents' existence, giving her even more reason to cling to him. Rebellion had been a heady experience.

She hadn't really meant to get pregnant. Or maybe she had, intending to use the pregnancy as a means of permanent escape from the proper, rigid life her parents imposed on her. Whatever, she and Daniel had intended to take responsibility for their actions. They'd planned to get married.

That's when the real trouble started. Her parents went ballistic. They insisted that Megan forget Daniel and go away someplace to have the baby—to save her reputation, they'd said—then put the child up for adoption. If she didn't fall in with their plans, they warned, she would find herself on the streets without a penny to her name the moment she turned eighteen. They also intended to have Daniel thrown in jail for rape.

The threatened retaliations against Daniel were what finally got through to Megan. Her father was a powerful man, and she'd had no doubt he could carry out those threats. So she and her parents reached a compromise. She would postpone her marriage to Daniel and go away to a maternity home in Oklahoma to have the baby, but she wouldn't consider adoption. She had loved the unborn child from the moment she'd known of its existence, and nothing and no one would take it away from her.

No one except God, that is.

She had returned home broken, physically spent and emotionally racked, looking forward to only one thing—her reunion with Daniel. He had written her sporadically over the past seven months, always saying how much he missed her, how much he loved her. But when she'd tried to call him, his number was disconnected. In a panic, she'd gone to the house he'd shared with his father, and found it empty.

Nothing much had mattered after that.

The buzz of the intercom brought Megan back to the present. She raked one hand over her face to clear her head, thinking that her brief trip down memory lane hadn't been as bad as she'd feared.

She pushed the intercom button. "Yes?"

"There's a...um, Mr. Ramsey here to see you."

Rage welled up inside her once again. How dare he? Could the man not take no for an answer? "Tell him I'm too busy."

She heard urgent whispering in the background. "It's a Mr. *Brian* Ramsey," the receptionist clarified.

Brian. Oh, Lord, she wasn't ready for this. But how could she turn him away, a child desperately seeking his mother? What had Holt told him? "I'll come get him."

She took a moment to wipe the mascara from under her eyes, evidence of the tears she hadn't even been aware she was shedding. Then she headed for the reception area, trying and failing to come up with just the right words.

Brian was a great kid, she thought, feeling another surge of anger toward Holt. If Holt was so intent on protecting his son from pain, he shouldn't have told Brian she was his mother until he was absolutely sure.

Brian was standing awkwardly by the door, looking as if he might flee at any moment. When he saw Megan, however, he stood up taller and thrust his chin out resolutely.

"Hello, Brian," she said with a tentative smile.

He didn't return the smile.

"My office is this way. Come on back." She turned, trusting he would follow. When they were alone in her office with the door closed, she gestured toward a chair, the same one his father had sat in one week ago, but Brian ignored it. He continued to stand, arms folded, staring at her with a combination of suspicion, anger and heartbreaking vulnerability.

"My dad told me there was some stupid mix-up," he began, "that you're not really my mother."

"I'm so sorry." She didn't know what else to say.

"Is that what you told him? That it was all a mistake?"

"It *was* a mistake," she said emphatically.

"I don't believe it. Look, I understand why you'd like to ignore me. You probably never thought I'd come looking for you—"

"Brian—"

He forged ahead, refusing to let her interrupt. "I want you to know that I don't plan to interfere in your life. You've made it real clear you don't want anything to do with me. But I just want you to tell me why—why you gave me up, and why you—"

"But I didn't give you up! Brian, I know how badly you want to find your birth mother, and I honestly wish I could be her. But there's been a mistake. I'm sure if you keep searching, everything will get straightened out and you'll find your real..." While she'd spoken, Brian had withdrawn a piece of paper from the back pocket of his jeans and tossed it onto her drawing board.

She was scared to death to pick it up.

"Go on, take a look," Brian urged. "Then tell me about mistakes."

Megan's hands trembled as she unfolded the piece of paper. It was a birth certificate, one that was hauntingly familiar to her in many ways. The date, time and place of birth, the attending physician's signature—all were the same as those listed on the birth certificate tucked away in her jewelry box at home. Under "Mother of Child," her own name stared back at her.

But there were some critical differences between the two documents. The child named on this certificate was male: "Boy Carlisle." And he had been born alive.

One other condition set this document apart from the one Megan had at home: this one was notarized. Danielle's birth certificate was only a photocopy.

The room began spinning, and Megan clutched at the edge of her drawing board for support.

"Ms. Carlisle? You okay?"

"I..." She managed to make it to her own chair without taking a nosedive onto the carpet. "I'm fine," she lied. "I can see now why you and your father were so sure. This document is very convincing, but it's simply not true. I gave birth to a girl. I had a daughter. Danielle."

"What happened to her?" Brian asked, all his earlier belligerence gone.

"She died." Megan was amazed, but the words weren't quite as devastating as before. "Actually, she never really lived. She was stillborn. And someone...well, I don't know why, but someone obviously doctored my daughter's birth certificate to produce this one." *Or Danielle's was the one that was phony.* The suspicion was inescapable.

Brian sank slowly into the other chair, a thoughtful expression on his earnest young face. "Then you don't think there's any chance you're..." He left the sentence unfinished.

"I don't see how I could be. Oh, Brian, I wish it were true. I would count myself really lucky to have given life to a great kid like you. But just because we're not related doesn't mean we can't be friends."

He studied her, perhaps gauging her sincerity. "Not if Dad has anything to say about it. You made him pretty mad. He didn't say so, but I know he thinks you're lying."

"Then I'll make him understand." For some reason, it was suddenly important that Holt not believe her to be a liar. "I'll give him a copy of my daughter's birth certificate. Maybe his private detective can figure out what happened, and that will help him find your real mother."

"Do you think so?" Brian asked, sounding less than enthusiastic.

"That's what you want, isn't it?"

He looked at her sheepishly. "I was kind of getting used to the idea that *you* were my mother. But, yeah, that's what I want, to find her and my natural father, too." He gave her a half smile, and her heart lurched.

Megan hoped she disguised her dismay by bustling down the hall to make a photocopy of Brian's birth certificate. Then, as quickly as she could, she sent him on his way with a promise that she would do her best to track down the truth. It was only when she was once again alone that she gave in to the feelings of panic.

She hadn't wanted to get Brian's hopes up again, only to have them dashed, but, God in heaven, what if it were true? What if Brian was her son? Was it even remotely possible? No, it couldn't be. No way.

Yes, it could be, she realized when she recalled that sheepish half smile Brian had flashed. When he smiled like that, tilting his head just so, he was the spitting image of Daniel Turner.

The day was turning into another scorcher, but Holt didn't mind the heat. The main reason he'd gotten into this business was to spend time outdoors in the sun and fresh air, but as his nurseries had multiplied, he'd spent more and more of his time behind a desk.

But today his newest location, in suburban Plano, demanded his back as well as his brain. The physical labor needed to move landscaping timbers actually felt good, and it served the dual purpose of keeping thoughts of Megan Carlisle at bay.

He was so damned disappointed in her. Just when he'd started to believe she might really be good for Brian, she'd up and proved that she was every bit as selfish as he'd feared from the beginning. He'd talked himself into believing that the story about a stillborn daughter was just a smoke screen to throw him off the track.

Then why had her tears seemed so genuine, her grief so real?

Even now, the thought of those big brown eyes, unnaturally shiny with tears, tugged at his heart.

Dammit, he was doing it again. He forced his attention back to the job at hand. "Let's do one more stack along the fence," he told the kid who was helping him.

"Uh, Mr. Ramsey? I don't mean to disagree with you, but it's August and not that many people are doing landscaping now. Are you sure we need to put out this many timbers?"

Holt took a second look at the display and cursed himself. He hadn't been paying the slightest bit of attention to what he was doing. Thoughts of Megan kept sneaking in, stealing his concentration. "You're right, Joe. We've got plenty here." He gave the kid a reassuring smile. "Don't ever be afraid to argue with the boss. I like for my employees to use their brains."

Joe grinned. "Yes, sir. I'll put the cart away and check on the sod. Want to keep it nice and wet in this heat."

Holt headed indoors, intending to pour himself a huge glass of ice tea. That's when he saw her, standing under a canopy of vines, looking as incredibly cool as a mirage in the desert. A patch of sunlight illuminated Megan's turquoise silk dress so that it shone like a gemstone, and her long hair was coiled loosely on top of her head, revealing the slender column of her neck.

He was staring at her, he realized, and she was staring right back at him.

"You're a hard man to track down," she said when he approached, his heart racing. "This is the third Ram Nursery I've visited trying to find you. I'd just missed you at the first two."

"I've been making the rounds." He pulled a bandanna from the back pocket of his jeans and wiped the sweat from his face and neck, wishing he didn't have to face her looking so…unpresentable. "What's the matter, Megan, did the guilt get to you?"

She looked up at the sky, down at the toes of her brightly colored sandals, anywhere but at him, and he could tell by the way her jaw clenched that she was trying to master her temper. "The only thing I regret is that I didn't let you show me this Saturday night. It explains a lot." She pulled a piece of paper from her purse and handed it to him.

Holt unfolded it, immediately recognizing it as Brian's birth certificate. "Where did you get this?" he asked suspiciously.

"Brian showed me the original, and I made a copy."

"Brian!" Holt exploded. "When did you see him?"

"This morning. He rode his bike to my office."

"Rode his—from Lakewood all the way to Oak Lawn? Good grief, has the kid lost his mind? I left him this morning quietly cleaning the pool, and…well, never mind. I guess that's not the point, is it?" He would deal with Brian later.

"The point is that I understand now why you were so sure I was Brian's mother."

"And you still maintain you're not?" Holt demanded, his voice rising a notch.

"Is there someplace private we could continue this discussion?" she asked. "I have something to show you, and then maybe you'll understand."

All Holt could understand right now was that, despite everything, he desired her. His hands itched to touch her silky-looking dress, to feel the warmth of her skin beneath the slick material, to feel the weight of her breasts against his palms. Several tendrils of her hair had escaped the knot on top of her head, trailing damply down her cheeks and around her ears. So, she wasn't immune to the heat after all.

"We can use the manager's office," he said gruffly, turning to lead the way.

Once inside the office, he reached into the small refrigerator and poured that ice tea he'd promised himself earlier. He only wished he could dump it over his head instead of merely drinking it. "You want some?" he asked belatedly, after taking several cooling swallows.

"No, thanks." She claimed the chair in front of the desk, daintily crossing her slim ankles. An air-conditioning window unit did its best to cool the office, stirring up a gentle breeze and causing Megan's perfume to tease the air around Holt.

Only after he'd drunk his fill of tea did he sit down behind the desk, deliberately choosing a position of authority. "Now, what was it you wanted to show me?"

She laid another folded piece of paper on the desktop. When Holt opened it, at first he assumed it was a second copy of Brian's birth certificate, until he examined it more closely. Suddenly his lungs couldn't hold quite enough oxygen.

Dear God, it was just as she'd claimed. She'd given birth to a girl—the same date, time and place as Brian, same doctor, but the baby had been female.

And she'd died.

He felt like an insensitive clod. "Then you really aren't Brian's mother."

She took a deep, audible breath. "I'm not sure anymore," she said, her voice trembling. She stood and paced the small office. "When I told you I was *there* when my baby was born, that wasn't entirely the truth. I had a cesarean, so I was under a general anesthetic. When I woke up, they told me my baby girl—" Her voice broke, and she turned away from him, furtively swiping at her eyes. "I'm sorry. After all these years, it shouldn't affect me like this."

Holt was out of his chair and around the desk in an instant. From behind her he placed his hands on her shoulders, wanting to do more but not daring to. "Please don't cry. I didn't mean to do this to you, Megan. I didn't mean to dredge up all this pain." Nothing undid him like a woman's tears.

Sometimes Shelley had cried when the pain was too intense, and he hated like hell the impotence he'd felt because he couldn't help her.

"Please don't cry," he repeated, rubbing his hands up and down Megan's arms. She was so fragile-feeling, and her hair smelled better than the most fragrant flower sold by his nursery. He wanted to press his face against that hair and test its softness. "I'm sorry for everything. Brian and I won't bother you anymore."

She pulled away suddenly, putting several paces between them. He thought at first that she might be angry over the liberties he'd taken, but when she turned and he saw the pinkness in her face, he realized she was embarrassed.

"Maybe I need to cry," she said, blinking rapidly. "I didn't at the time. I just felt dry and empty inside." She fished in her purse for a tissue. He turned his attention toward the desk, straightening papers, giving her a chance to compose herself.

"Anyway," she said a few moments later, her voice much steadier, "the more I think about it, the more uncertain I become about what really happened fourteen years ago. I don't remember my baby's birth. I never even saw her. They said it would be better if I didn't.

"There was no funeral—nothing. My parents insisted that it would be best if I put the 'incident' behind me. Incident. They referred to her as an incident, like she wasn't a real person. And, God help me, maybe she wasn't."

"Are you saying your daughter's birth certificate might have been faked?"

She winced and bit her lower lip, then shook her head emphatically. "No, it just couldn't be. That would mean my parents lied to me, and the doctor—and two nuns. My father, especially, was dead-set against my keeping the baby, and he was powerful enough to bend a lot of people to his will, but I can't imagine him making *nuns* lie."

"Everyone has a price, or a button that can be pushed—even nuns." Holt paused, wondering if he should tell her the rest. He hesitated to cause her any more pain. But he sensed that she'd been completely honest with him; he owed her the same courtesy. "There's something else you should know. I have Brian's adoption papers, including the consent form. It has your notarized signature on it."

She shook her head in denial. "I never signed any such form."

"Could you have signed something not knowing what it was?"

"I don't know. Those first few days after the birth, I was in kind of a fog. But I suppose my signature could have been forged, the notary seal faked. Whoever mocked up the phony birth certificate could have done it."

She turned toward him suddenly, the full horror of what they were discussing registered in her eyes. "My God, listen to us! We're talking like it's true. But it's just too fantastic. There must be another explanation."

He felt a momentary surge of resentment toward her. "Would it be so bad to find out Brian is your son?"

She shook her head. "No, of course not. As far as kids go, I couldn't do better than Brian." She looked at Holt quizzically. "You don't get it, do you?"

"I'm afraid I don't."

"Well, there's no sense discussing this further until we find out for sure. I can think of only one person who might know the truth—my mother."

"Then let's go see her."

Megan shook her head. "*I'll* go see her. You have to understand—my mother and I are barely on speaking terms. She won't be pleased to see me, and certainly not with a stranger in tow. Although..."

"Although what?" he asked, thinking privately that Megan Carlisle certainly hadn't lived the easy life Benny Powell had described.

She actually managed a mischievous, though watery, smile. "Mother has always been somewhat in awe of men, all men. Your presence might just lend a needed air of authority to the occasion. She might not confide in me, but with you there to intimidate..."

"Hey, I'm not in the business of intimidating women."

Megan's eyebrows flew up. "No? You did a pretty good job with me. Anyway, you won't have to do a thing. Just stand there and act like she owes you something. She'll crumble like a shortbread cookie."

He wasn't particularly comfortable with that image, but what could he do? He'd already volunteered to go with Megan when she confronted her mother. "Okay, when?" he asked.

"Tonight, around seven?"

He nodded. After making arrangements to pick her up at her Oak Lawn apartment, he walked her to her Jeep, his hands rigidly at his sides. He wouldn't make the mistake of touching her again. "Say, Megan, about the kitchen..."

"I'll understand if you don't want me to do it."

"I'll understand if you don't *want* to do it. You said you would turn it over to that Sheena person if you discovered anything underhanded going on, which there was. If that's what you decide to do, I'll go along with it. But I'd still like for you to be involved."

Her eyes lit up, and she offered him the first genuine smile he'd seen from her that day. "Really? You mean, you really want your kitchen remodeled?"

"Well, I didn't at first, but after I saw the plans you drew up, I changed my mind."

"I see." She reached into her Jeep, pulled an envelope off the front seat and handed it to him. "Here's the estimate. I prepared it, just in case."

As he watched her drive off, Holt wondered if he was plain crazy. He could hardly keep his hands off the woman, and he'd just invited her to spend the next few weeks underfoot in his kitchen. What if it turned out that she *was* Brian's mother?

Originally, Holt had planned to carefully monitor the contact between Brian and Megan. With her hanging around the remodeling, that plan would go right out the window.

He supposed he could always change his mind about the kitchen on the pretext that her estimate was too high. But hadn't he already lied to the woman enough? He didn't think he could be anything but truthful from now on, with one exception: he wouldn't let her know how much he wanted her.

Five

When Megan got home from work later that day, she peeled off the sticky silk shirtwaist and liberally doused her body with baby powder, wishing she had time for a shower. But Holt would arrive in a few minutes, and her place was a wreck. He'd already seen her office looking like a hazardous waste dump and her Jeep window-deep in debris from her work. He didn't need to know that she lived the same way at home.

After donning white denim shorts, a neon orange T-shirt and matching Keds, she ran around her living room scooping up piles of folders, sketchpads, clipboards and sample books and tossed them into her bedroom. It took seven trips, but soon she had things looking relatively neat.

Unfortunately, no matter how thoroughly she cleaned, she couldn't make the place any classier. Her apartment was in a gracious but slightly seedy old building in a neighborhood that could best be described as checkered. The apartment had benefits, like high ceilings, big windows, hardwood floors—and drawbacks, like peeling plaster, rusty plumbing and archaic air-conditioning. Through careful purchases at flea markets and estate sales, she'd managed a sort of funky chic...well, that might be giving the decor a little more credit than it deserved.

Although she'd never considered money and the things it could buy to be a priority in her life, she'd lived with wealth too long not to appreciate some of its trappings. She didn't want much: just a bathtub big enough to stretch out in, a kitchen big enough to turn around in, a king-size brass bed big enough to—

Stop that!

As she quickly dusted the antique trunk that served as her coffee table, it occurred to her that she was going to a lot of trouble for no good reason. Why would Holt care what her apartment looked like? *His* home wasn't exactly a decorating sensation—not yet, anyway. So what if he thought she was a tasteless slob? It shouldn't matter.

But it did.

When she'd first seen Holt this afternoon, unloading those big timbers from a cart, she'd felt a primal tug deep inside, along with a white heat that had nothing to do with the scorching summer sun. He'd been wearing faded jeans and a royal blue knit shirt that had revealed his every muscle to perfection as he'd lifted and lowered the heavy slabs of wood. Holt Ramsey had looked as tanned and strong and virile as a man could get, and the memory made her hot and gave her goose bumps all at the same time.

Even watching him glug down a glass of ice tea, his throat rippling rhythmically, had been a sensual experience. And when he'd touched her...

He'd meant only to comfort her, but her body hadn't understood his intentions. Her tears had been quickly forgotten as another biological urge took over. A swirling coil of heat had formed in the pit of her stomach, urging her to turn, to touch, to arouse as she'd been aroused. She'd done well to step away from him when she did.

Dear Lord, what if she really was Brian's mother? The possibility was almost too wonderful and too terrible to contemplate. Her attraction to Holt, her client, was bad enough, but for her to be lusting after her son's adopted father—that would be just too awful! The potential complications boggled her mind.

Her doorbell rang, and she threw her bottle of furniture polish and her dust rag under the couch before buzzing Holt through the security entrance downstairs. Moments later he was knocking at her door. She pasted on a smile and let him in.

"You're early," she said, although the old carriage clock on her bookcase read precisely seven o'clock.

"I didn't think I was," he replied with a shrug. "How do you always manage to look so cool when the rest of the city is melting like wax in this heat?"

"Lots of baby powder," she confessed, thinking that Holt looked pretty cool himself, although she wasn't about to say so. She absolutely would *not* flirt with him, no matter how tempting he looked, no matter how good an opening he'd given her. "Let me grab my purse and we can go."

"I like your place," he said as she searched for her keys. "It . . . suits you."

"Thank you," she replied, not sure whether she'd been complimented or not. Still, the fact that he'd noticed it at all pleased her. Ah, there were her keys, on the windowsill.

The afternoon heat was letting up now, Megan noticed as they walked outdoors. The slight breeze actually felt good, cooling the damp nape of her neck. "Do you mind if we take your car? Mine is, er . . ."

"I've seen it. Have you applied for disaster relief?"

"It's not *that* bad," she huffed, although actually it was. Any passenger brave enough to ride in her Jeep would have to sit on her dry cleaning, which she'd been meaning to drop off for several days. "I suppose your car is immaculate?"

Then stopped in front of his Porsche, and she could see that it was. He'd probably just had it washed and detailed. He grinned and said nothing.

She rested one hand lightly on the sleek car's dark green hood and sighed. "I love your car, by the way. My father had one of these. He only let me ride in it once. I never even bothered asking if I could drive it."

"You want to drive mine?" Holt asked as casually as he would have offered the loan of a pen.

"Oh, no, I mean—"

"Here, go ahead." He tossed her the keys.

"Are you sure?"

"You're a careful driver, aren't you?"

She could tell him she drove the same way she managed her life. That might give him pause. But she merely nodded and moved to the driver's side of the car.

The first thing she noticed as she slid behind the wheel was that the car smelled like him—like leather and saddle soap. The seat was firm and felt good against her body. She moved it forward several notches so she could reach the pedals. Then she adjusted the mirrors, donned her sunglasses, fastened her seat belt. Finally she inserted the key into the ignition and thrilled as the powerful engine roared to life.

A sideways glance told her that Holt was amused by her excitement. Well, she didn't care. She was going to enjoy herself.

The car was a pure pleasure to drive, responsive to the slightest pressure on the gas, agile on turns, the gearshift moving as smoothly as a spoon in cake batter. She caressed the glossy wooden shift knob with one hand, the fleece-wrapped steering wheel in the other, and even noticed the feel of the leather, soft as whipped cream, against the back of her thighs.

The whole experience was so sensory, the only thing she could think of that equaled it was making love.

At a red light she chanced another glance and saw Holt watching her, his expression inscrutable. Lord, she hoped he couldn't read minds.

"So where does your mother live, anyway?" he asked, breaking the silence.

Megan came down to earth with a plunk as she suddenly remembered where she was supposed to be going and why.

Odd, but for a moment there she'd actually forgotten, pretending she and Holt were going out on a date or something. But Holt didn't date, she reminded herself, and they were on their way to visit her mother so they could find out whether Megan's child had lived or died.

"My mother lives on Strait Lane," she finally managed. Hoping Holt didn't catch on that they'd been headed in the wrong direction, she took a right at the corner and then another right. She felt slightly sick to her stomach.

Holt noticed the abrupt change in her mood and cursed himself for having said anything. For the first time since he'd alerted Megan to the possibility that she might be Brian's mother, she'd been smiling, happy, driving his car with her usual verve. She'd made a sexy package with that secret smile, hiding behind the dark lenses of her shades, the wind whipping unruly strands from the hair piled on top of her head.

And her skin...ever since she'd mentioned baby powder, he'd been fighting off a persistent mental image of his hand gliding over Megan's smooth, powdered skin.

He shouldn't have said anything. He should have just let her drive, all the way to Mexico if she'd wanted. He would have enjoyed the ride, just watching her and fantasizing.

But now that he'd opened Pandora's box, he wasn't willing to simply drop it. "Is visiting your mother always this stressful for you? Or are you worried about what she might tell you?"

The light turned green. She stepped on the gas and the car shot forward. "Both, I guess."

"What's the deal with you and your mother? Unless you'd rather not talk about it."

"I don't mind. It's all ancient history as far as I'm concerned, but Mother won't let it go. The whole thing boils down to the fact that I didn't live my life the way my parents wanted me to. They had everything mapped out, from my education to the number and sex of my future children. A pregnancy at age seventeen wasn't on their list."

"Megan, that was fourteen years ago. How long can someone hold a grudge?"

"Oh, there was more. After the pregnancy, I behaved for a while—went to the college they wanted after Dad pulled a lot of strings, pledged my mom's sorority and married an acceptable man. Darren Clemson was cash poor, but he had an impeccable pedigree."

Good God, it sounded like Megan's parents thought of her more as a prized poodle than a daughter.

"Yeah, everyone told me I was one lucky girl to catch Darren, under the circumstances."

Holt couldn't miss the bitterness in her voice. He knew he should probably drop the subject, but he was thirsty for knowledge about Megan Carlisle. He wanted to know why she seemed so fragile at times.

"So Clemson was a real prince, huh?" he ventured.

Megan snorted. "Hardly. He was an egotistical male chauvinist pig . . . and a bully."

His chest ached at the thought of gentle Megan being saddled with such an undeserving husband. "Then why'd you marry him?"

"I don't know. Honestly, I don't know how I could have been so stupid. I wanted to please my parents, I suppose. I kept vainly trying to prove to them that I hadn't ruined my life."

"How long were you married?"

"Five years. It worked for a while, as long as I was a good little wife. But somewhere along the line I woke up and realized I had a life to lead. And when Darren wouldn't let me lead it, I left him."

Holt had a feeling she was leaving out an awful lot. Someday he might press her, but not now. Her emotional plate was pretty full at the moment.

"Anyway, the divorce didn't go over real well with the folks. They said it just proved what they'd known all along, that I was foolish and ungrateful and unworthy of their blood. Sometimes they acted like they wanted to forgive me, but there were always conditions attached to their forgiveness. They never stopped trying to get me back under their thumbs."

She paused, pretending to study the street signs. "One day I made my father particularly angry, and that night he had a heart attack. He went to his grave cursing me, and he told Mother that if she wanted to join him in heaven someday, she'd better take over the cursing where he left off."

"And she did?" Holt asked, amazed.

Megan nodded. "I can't recall that Mother ever went against my father, or disagreed with him or crossed him in any way. She was raised to believe that men were always right. She's loyal to him, I'll give her that."

"What happened to your ex?"

"When he realized he couldn't get anything from me in the settlement—there was nothing to get—he drifted off and snagged the heiress to an electronics empire. I suspected all along that he'd married me for my family's money, and he more or less admitted it after the divorce."

An illogical rage filled Holt at the thought of anyone using Megan that way. He wanted to find that slimy slug of an ex-husband of hers and pound his face in. "Are you telling me," Holt said in slow, measured tones, "that your parents faulted you for dumping a jerk like that?"

She shrugged. "The divorce embarrassed them, just like the pregnancy did." She obviously caught his unguarded reaction to her words, because she added, "Don't let it bother you. I've come to terms with it. Of course it's a shame that Dad and I didn't reconcile before he died. At one time we were very close, but...well, the timing was bad. And someday Mother will come around. She's getting softer all the time. She even sent me a birthday card this year."

Megan's outwardly cavalier attitude didn't fool Holt. There was a certain stiffness around her mouth and an almost desperate carelessness in her voice that belied her words. Her parents' harsh treatment of her had cut her deeply.

How could anyone turn away their one and *only* child? Holt couldn't imagine turning his back on Brian, no matter what the circumstances.

In a purely reflexive gesture, he laid his hand gently over hers where it rested on the gearshift. She looked over at him, startled, then returned her attention to the road without comment. But she left her hand where it was.

Holt's first glimpse of the Carlisle estate took his breath away. Outside of "Lifestyles of the Rich and Famous," did people really live this way? Through a wrought-iron gate, he could see the redbrick driveway meandering under a canopy of towering oaks, past a fountain, to a majestic Colonial house with gleaming white columns. All the scene needed was a little Spanish moss draped here and there to pass for *Gone With the Wind*'s Tara.

Megan had stopped before the gate and was speaking into an intercom. "Tell her I have important business." She turned to Holt. "Her curiosity will get the better of her, if nothing else, and she'll see me."

"You mean there's a chance she might turn you away?"

"She might. I've never tried dropping in unannounced before."

After what seemed like a long wait, the gates swung silently open as if guided by an invisible hand. Megan pulled the car brazenly up to the front door and cut the engine.

She handed Holt the keys. "Thanks for letting me drive. It was a . . . diverting experience."

The mansion came equipped with a butler. The stuffy little man escorted Holt and Megan through the front door into a white, marble-tiled foyer. From there they were led to a cozy, feminine sitting room overrun with flowery chintz and ruffles. Megan flopped down with casual disregard for the pristine furnishings, while Holt perched gingerly on the edge of his chair. Although he couldn't deny that he was now wealthy himself, he hadn't been raised that way. He still wasn't entirely comfortable around any sort of ostentation.

The grande dame of the house appeared a few moments later, a petite, dark-haired woman like her daughter, dressed in a flowing silk kimono, but that was where the resemblance ended. Mrs. Carlisle had a cool, regal bearing, a sense of imperviousness, whereas Megan was as touchable as a rag doll.

Holt realized with a start that he knew Mrs. Carlisle. Or rather, he'd met her once, at some charity event or other. He sometimes got rooked into attending such affairs, but he seldom paid attention to all the people he met.

"Mother," Megan said, rising to her feet, looking like she wanted to take her mother's hand or kiss her cheek or *something,* but she didn't.

"Megan. You're looking fit."

Megan put a self-conscious hand to her wind-mussed hair. "Um, Mother, this is Holt Ramsey. He—"

"Mr. Ramsey!" The older woman's face creased into an unexpected smile. "Why, of course. We met at the Cystic Fibrosis Ball, don't you remember? You were with that charming Grace Bonwinn."

"Yes, I remember. How are you, Mrs. Carlisle?" he asked politely, wondering how the woman could possibly recall Grace Bonwinn when Holt himself couldn't.

"Call me Rolanda, please. Have you two had dinner? I believe my chef is preparing—"

"Mother, this isn't really a social call," Megan said sharply.

Rolanda's lips pursed in irritation. "Oh, yes. You said something about business. Well, sit down, sit down, and tell me what this is all about."

Megan wasted no time reaching into her purse and pulling out the two birth certificates. She handed them both to Rolanda, then plopped back into her chair and fidgeted with the hem of her shorts as she waited for her mother's inevitable reaction.

Holt was none-too-calm, either, but he was more concerned with how Megan would handle the outcome than with the actual outcome itself. She looked like she was ready to shatter.

After an interminable amount of time, Rolanda looked up. "What is this supposed to mean?"

"We thought you could tell us. I'm sure you recognize one birth certificate as your granddaughter's. The other one, 'Boy Carlisle,' belongs to Holt's adopted son, Brian. Since I didn't give birth to twins..." She let her voice trail off.

Rolanda turned accusing eyes on Holt. "Where did you get this?" she demanded, shaking the piece of paper.

"I petitioned a judge to unseal Brian's adoption records. I have the notarized copy at home."

"That's not possible!" Rolanda turned to her daughter. "Megan, I can't believe you fell for this. This is obviously some sort of scheme to get to our money. Documents can be faked, you know."

Megan rose out of her chair. "That's exactly the point! Documents can be faked. But which one? I never saw Danielle's original birth certificate, or even a notarized copy. For that matter, I never saw Danielle. But I've seen Brian. He's a handsome, healthy fourteen-year-old who wants to find his birth mother. It has nothing to do with money, believe me."

Rolanda stood also, and her face paled beneath her artfully applied makeup. "What are you trying to say?"

"I should think that would be obvious. I wanted to keep my baby. You and Dad didn't want me to. As usual, you got your way, and my feelings didn't matter." With each word Megan had moved closer to her mother, until now the two women were almost nose to nose. "I bore a healthy boy, and you lied to me and told me I'd given birth to a girl who died."

"That's not true!" Rolanda shook her head in denial. "How could you even think I would do that to my own daughter?"

"I can easily see you doing it, if you thought it would make your lives easier, if you thought it was for my own good. And you *always* knew what was best for me, didn't you? Marrying me off to Darren was a shining example of your good judgment.''

Rolanda's red-tinged lips tightened into a thin line as she reclaimed her chair along with her control. "I think we can all agree that Darren was a mistake.''

"A mistake? How about a catastrophe? Did you know I almost killed myself because of him?" When her mother's eyes widened in shock, Megan continued relentlessly. "I saved up three bottles of those sleeping pills that quack doctor of yours prescribed. But I was too much of a coward.''

Holt gripped the arms of his chair to prevent himself from jumping between the two women. He wasn't sure what he'd expected to happen when Megan confronted her mother, but this wasn't it. He'd wanted to learn more about what made Megan tick, but he was learning too much too fast. He felt like an eavesdropper listening in on a conversation that wasn't meant for his ears.

"Excuse me," he said, and his interruption jarred both women, because they turned and stared at him like they'd forgotten he was there. "I think we should get back to the subject of Megan's child. Is it possible, Mrs. Carlisle, that your husband deceived Megan without your knowledge?''

"My husband did not lie to me," she said, recovering her regal bearing.

"Oh, please," Megan objected as she paced the room. "He lied to you all the time. What about when he had that affair—''

"Megan! I will not have you speaking ill of your father when he's not here to defend himself.''

"He doesn't need to be here. He has you to defend him. You're so blindly loyal to him, you can't admit that he was far from perfect.''

"No one is perfect," Rolanda shot back. "And there's nothing wrong with loyalty. Look, both of you," she said in a calmer voice, including Holt. "There's an easy way to solve this. Cramer kept a file on you, Megan, and I'm sure Danielle's notarized birth certificate is in there. We'll all just go to the library and see for ourselves." She turned and glided out of the parlor.

Holt took Megan's hand when she would have charged after her mother like a rhinoceros. "Try to take it easy, huh?" he whispered. "This isn't easy for any of us."

"Yeah, right," she huffed under her breath. But she did seem to calm down a little.

Rolanda led them across the foyer and into a room with fourteen-foot ceilings and floor-to-ceiling bookshelves. Those shelves were lined with all matter of leather-bound volumes, some obviously ancient. A massive mahogany desk, resting on a thick antique Oriental carpet, dominated the room. Ledger books, pens, a magnifying glass and other paraphernalia of Cramer Carlisle's work sat on the dustless surface, as if their owner had just stepped away from the desk for a few moments. It was kind of eerie.

Rolanda walked directly to an oak filing cabinet and pulled open the second drawer. She searched until she found the file she sought, then laid it on the desk and opened it, quickly riffling through the contents. The file contained bits and pieces of Megan's past—programs from school recitals, childish watercolor paintings, ribbons from horse shows and tennis matches.

Finally Rolanda found the elusive document. She pulled it out of the folder with a flourish. "See, there, I told you. The notarized copy of Danielle's birth certificate. I think you owe your father an apology."

Megan stared mutely at the piece of paper. Holt couldn't imagine what was going through her head, but there was a definite look of relief in her eyes, though it was tinged with sadness.

Holt felt his own hopes evaporating. Apart from wanting to find Brian's mother for him, he wanted to give Megan back the child she'd lost. He took the certificate from Megan's nerveless grasp and examined it himself.

"Wait a minute."

Two sets of brown eyes stared at him.

He switched on the desk lamp, picked up the magnifying glass and scrutinized the document more carefully. "It's been altered. See, how when I hold it up against the light, some areas of the paper are thicker?"

He began painstakingly chipping away at the thin coating of white that covered up the document's original entries. Before long, his efforts put an end to their speculation. Megan had given birth to a live baby boy, and someone, most likely her father, had gone to great lengths to conceal the truth from her.

"Dear God," Rolanda murmured as she clutched the back of the desk chair for support. Her reaction was the most honest Holt had seen from her, and he had no doubts that until this moment she'd been ignorant of the cruel charade perpetrated on her daughter.

Megan, however, was too blinded by her own reaction to notice. "How could you?" she said in a voice so low and deadly, it reminded Holt of a she-wolf's growl. "How could you take from me something so precious? Your own grandson, for God's sake! How could you blithely turn him over to complete strangers to raise?"

Rolanda shook her head. "Megan, I..." But her voice cracked as tears filled her eyes.

Holt looked to Megan, hoping to see some compassion in her face. But he saw only unreasoning anger, and he supposed he couldn't blame her.

Perhaps it wasn't his place to interfere, but he did anyway. He couldn't watch mother and daughter tear into each other again. "Come on," he said, taking Megan's hand and all but dragging her away. "We found out what we came here for. Let's go. Good night, Mrs. Carlisle."

For a moment he thought Megan would fight him, but in the end she drooped like a wilted flower and he led her easily through the front door, guarded by the openly curious butler, and to the car.

Six

Megan was quiet on the way back to her apartment, but it wasn't a calm sort of quiet. She fiddled with her ring, worried a loose strand of hair and chewed on her lower lip. An almost palpable tension surrounded her like a force field.

When she finally did speak, she startled Holt. "Thank you," she said.

"For what?"

"For dragging me out of there when you did, before I could say or do something that couldn't be forgiven." She shuddered. "I've never in my life felt such raw, out-of-control anger. I didn't think I was capable of anything like that."

Holt understood. He had once lost control like that, almost punching Shelley's doctor. He had felt unreasoning rage toward the man who, in Holt's mind, had allowed Shelley to die. "I guess we don't know what we're capable of, until we're pushed to our limits."

"But all day long, I've suspected the truth. I went over and over it in my head, preparing myself to discover that Brian was really my son, and Danielle just a fantasy. And yet when I was faced with the reality, I was still shocked." She paused, then added, "For a minute, there, I actually hated my mother."

"Megan..." He hesitated to say anything that might recall her raw fury. But he had to speak his mind. "I don't think your mother knew. Unless she's an awfully good actress, she was as shocked and repulsed by that doctored birth certificate, and what it meant, as you were."

"Maybe," Megan conceded.

"Don't you think you were a little hard on her?"

"No."

"No?"

"If she was ignorant of the facts, it's only because she chose to be. She turned a blind eye to a lot of things. She let Dad send me off to that dreadful maternity home in Oklahoma without lifting a finger."

"Are you saying she could have prevented what happened?"

"That's exactly what I'm saying."

"If she'd known about the deceit, don't you think she would have stopped it?"

That gave Megan pause. "I don't know."

As he pulled into the parking lot, Holt still believed Megan had been too rough on her mother. But that was something she would have to work through by herself. And, really, it was none of his business. His main responsibility was to Brian.

"You don't have to come in," Megan said as he started to open his door.

"The hell I don't." He wasn't about to leave her like this, like a volcano dormant after an eruption, but poised for a second explosion.

"I'll be okay, really." Her sudden brightness rang false.

He didn't argue, but he followed her resolutely toward the front entrance of the old stucco building. "We still have some business to discuss. Like what to tell Brian."

She stopped midstride, giving a little gasp. "Brian."

"Yeah, remember him?" Frankly, he was having rather a hard time understanding Megan's attitude. Of course she was entitled to be angry, but it seemed to him that her joy at finding the child she'd lost would overshadow the anger.

"I guess for a little while I *did* forget him," she murmured as she started walking again, head down, fishing in her purse for her keys. "Too focused on myself, I guess."

Her apartment was hot and stuffy. Mechanically she dropped her purse on the floor, flipped the air-conditioning to high and headed for the kitchen. "You want something cold to drink? Ice tea, maybe?"

Holt followed her into the tiny kitchen and found her standing before the open refrigerator, her face a blank, as if she'd forgotten why she opened the door in the first place.

He closed it and swiveled her around to face him, resting his hands lightly on her shoulders. "There's no need for you to be so damn strong, you know. I can't begin to guess what you're feeling right now, but I can tell you're trying awfully hard to keep it inside. You don't have to do that. I won't think any less of you if you want to yell and scream and punch pillows."

"I'm fine, honestly. I think I got all the anger out of my system. I mean, how much more could there be?"

"Years' worth, I imagine."

She looked up at him, her huge brown eyes showing confusion and indecision. Then all at once those eyes welled up with tears and her composure crumpled.

Without a second thought he pulled her to him, wrapping his arms around her, trying to surround her with comfort. Violent sobs racked her body and her tears soaked the front of his shirt.

Holt felt helpless. He had expected her to cry, but not like this, not with this overwhelming sadness. He stroked her back, murmuring soothing words that were having no effect. He pulled the pins out of her hair, allowing what was left of the topknot to tumble over the backs of his hands. He finger-combed the thick, glossy strands, massaged her scalp and the back of her neck, where her tension had stubbornly settled.

She was soft everywhere he was hard, and she smelled like baby powder. Holt pressed his cheek against the top of her head and inhaled, noting with keen awareness that her hair bore a different scent, light and lemony.

About the same time he realized Megan's sobs were letting up, he acknowledged his own totally inappropriate feelings of desire for her. Given their proximity, she probably noticed it, too.

That's all they needed—to bring sex into an already-complicated situation.

Determinedly, he detached himself, gently setting her away from him. He tore a paper towel from the roll sitting on the countertop and handed it to her, all the while attempting to harness his libido.

"If you were a real gentleman, like Cary Grant, you'd have a hanky for me."

He had to admire her spunk. "Guess I'm just not a hanky kind of guy."

"You should have left when you had the chance. Look, I've gotten mascara all over your shirt."

"I'm sure it'll wash out."

"I'm so embarrassed. Tonight you've seen me at my worst, totally devoid of dignity."

"Dignity is overrated, anyway. Hey, why don't you go sit down and I'll get us those drinks?"

She nodded, still blotting her damp cheeks with the paper towel as she left him alone in the kitchen.

Holt opened the refrigerator and found an almost empty pitcher of ice tea and a half bottle of white wine. The wine seemed refreshing. He grabbed the bottle and, finding no wineglasses, poured them each a hefty amount in plastic tumblers.

The living room was starting to cool off. Megan was curled up on one end of the sofa, her feet tucked under her. She managed a weak smile when Holt handed her the wine.

She took a long sip. "Mmm. Not elegant, but effective."

Holt sat down next to her. "Feeling better?"

"A little."

He couldn't help touching her. He lifted a strand of her hair, testing its softness between thumb and forefinger. "Megan, do you remember what you said Saturday night at my house?"

"I said of lot of things."

"I mean about Brian. When I first told you I thought you were his mother, you said you were sorry that you weren't. Did you mean that?"

She stared at him, her brow furrowed, and then she nodded as comprehension dawned. "You mean, am I happy that Brian really is my son? And shouldn't I be jumping up and down with joy or something?"

"Well, something. I've been hoping all along that you were the right one, partly for Brian's sake, but mainly for yours. I wanted to give back what was taken from you."

She turned away, her knuckles pressed to her mouth.

"Oh, Megan, please don't cry again. I never meant to...to make you feel so awful. I'm just trying to understand."

She took a couple of deep breaths and turned back to face him, once again under control, although her eyes were suspiciously shiny. "How would you feel if you found out your own father stole your child from you? I'll never be able to think of him in the same way."

Holt nodded, conceding the point. He supposed his views of the situation were too simplistic.

"Then there's Danielle. For years I grieved for a daughter who never existed. Not a day went by that I didn't wonder what she would have looked like if she'd lived, whether she would have been pretty and smart, whether she would have become a great pianist, or an astronaut. And now it's like she died all over again, because she was never real."

"But there's Brian," Holt reminded her. "He's real."

"Yes, he's real," she agreed. "And I've missed the first fourteen years of his life. I never held him in my arms or fed him a bottle. I missed his first words, his first steps, his first day at school."

Holt was beginning to understand, and he felt like an idiot because she'd had to spell out the obvious. "Think of the future, Megan, not the past. Brian has lots of firsts left—his first day of high school, his first date, his... his first varsity soccer game. You'll be there for those."

"Will I?"

"You can see him as much as you want." She would never know how hard it was to give her that. All along he'd been worried that Brian's birth mother would somehow replace Shelley in Brian's heart, and here he was, giving Megan full permission to step in and take over. But what other choice did he have? She deserved a chance with Brian.

"I'll never be his mother," she said glumly. "Not really. Shelley was the one he called Mom, and that'll never change. I'll always be just a poor substitute."

He didn't know how to put her mind at ease on that count, so he said nothing.

She sighed. "I just thought of something else. Daniel. He ought to know that he has a child."

"Do you know where Daniel Turner is?" Holt asked, almost afraid of her answer. She had spoken her former lover's name with so much fondness. Until now, Holt hadn't thought much about the man who'd fathered Brian—the man who'd been Megan's lover. It disturbed him to picture Megan in an intimate relationship, disturbed him more than he liked.

She shook her head. "I lost track of Daniel a long time ago. When I came home from Oklahoma, the Turners had moved away and left no forwarding address. I never understood that. I mean, Daniel and his dad were drifters, so it doesn't surprise me that they moved on, but I never understood why he didn't tell me where they went."

"And you never saw him again?" Holt was ashamed at the relief he felt.

"No. My father said he would try to track him down, but I doubt he followed through, and I didn't press him. It would have been hard to face Daniel and tell him our baby had died."

"Did you love him?" Holt didn't know why that should matter, but it did.

"Yes."

"Would you like to see him again?"

Megan's eyebrows flew up. "Do *you* know where he is?"

"Not yet, but the same P.I. who found you is looking for Daniel. Brian wanted to meet both of his birth parents."

"I would like to see him again," she said, that fondness returning to her voice. "I've always wondered how he turned out."

Holt abhorred the jealousy he felt, but he couldn't seem to tamp it down. He wanted Megan to look at *him* that way, to say his name with that lilt in her voice and the mistiness in her eyes. He wanted to make love to her for hours on end, days, even, until she forgot Daniel's touch, and the touch of any other man, for that matter.

The force of his desire took him by surprise. It wasn't just simple lust, either; that, he could understand and control. What astounded him was the sudden possessiveness he felt for her, the tender protectiveness.

He wasn't sure when it had happened, but somewhere along the way he'd put his arm around her—to comfort her, no doubt, but her nearness wasn't making him comfortable. Neither was the way she was looking up at him with those guileless eyes, or the fact that her breath quickened when he tightened his grip on her shoulder.

He squeezed her shoulder again, just to see if he'd imagined her response. He hadn't. She tilted her chin up slightly and moistened her lips with the tip of her tongue. He lowered his head by slow increments, until he could feel the warmth of her breath on his face. Then he felt those soft, moist lips against his, and his every brain cell short-circuited.

Megan had no idea how it had happened. One minute they'd been talking about Daniel, the next she'd found herself trapped by Holt's mesmerizing gaze, pulled inexorably to him like a formless pile of metal shavings to a magnet.

She could think of a thousand and one reasons she shouldn't allow this to go on, but not one of them was compelling enough to make her pull away from his intoxicating kiss. He made it so easy to forget everything and just dive into the inviting realm of smell and taste and touch.

Her body sprang to life, her response evoking physical sensations she had forgotten existed. Her breasts ached for Holt's hands, her skin tingled and a roiling heat swirled at the core of her being, reminding her how very long she had denied herself the pleasures a man could bring.

She reached up with one tentative hand and touched his hair, his neck, to finally fasten her grip on his collar. He deepened the kiss, delving into her mouth with his tongue. She heard a tortured moan and realized it came from her own throat.

It was Holt who eventually ended the kiss, breaking away suddenly, although he continued to hold her against him. "That was not the smartest thing I've ever done," he murmured, almost to himself.

She had to agree. But some selfish, needy part of her refused to let him go, or make it any easier for him to pull away. She didn't care about what was sensible or prudent. She only wanted to cling to him, to let him fill all the parts of her soul that felt so empty right now. He was the only one who understood what she'd gone through.

"Don't go," she whispered. If he left, she would be alone, and she would have to face all the demons that waited for her. If he stayed, he could keep them at bay, at least for a while.

"We'd be crazy to take this any further," he said, not sounding quite like the confident, sure-voiced man she was accustomed to.

"I always knew I was crazy."

"You're not crazy. But you've had a helluva day. I doubt you're in the best state of mind to make a decision like..."

His voice trailed off as she planted a series of light kisses along his neck, ending with a nip just inside his collar.

God, he smelled good. She couldn't put a name to the scent, but if she could bottle it, she'd make millions.

"You're playing with fire, lady." Despite the reprimand in his voice, he began to caress her back with slow, sinuous strokes. The hem of her shirt had pulled loose from the back of her shorts, and he slipped his hand beneath the orange fabric to touch bare skin.

She shivered at the contact. Her whole body was pulsing to the frantic beat of her heart. "I like fire," she murmured before pulling his head down and sealing her mouth against his. And she was burning inside with the fire he'd kindled to life. The flames chased away those cold caverns of pain and disillusionment.

She could feel it the instant he abandoned all hesitation. One minute he was holding back, the next he nearly overwhelmed her with the strength of his desire, which hovered around them and between them like an entity unto itself. Holt delved into her mouth with his tongue, one hand holding her at the back of her neck, a willing captive, the other boldly exploring every curve of her body.

Bullets of excitement shot through her body as he touched her breast, her abdomen, her thigh. His nimble fingers slid up the leg of her shorts to tease the lace edge of her panties.

"Do you have any idea what you do to me?" he said on a groan as he pushed her back onto the sofa cushions and covered her body with his, hot and heavy and powerfully male. "I've never wanted any woman like I want you. But I can't stand the thought of hurting you—"

"You won't hurt me. I need this. I need you. Badly." It wasn't just the physical release she craved, either. She'd meant it when she said she needed *him*. Holt Ramsey. A good, decent man who had seen her pain and, she was sure, had felt it with her.

There were no further words between them as urgency took precedence. Clothes were flung in all directions. Although she had never undressed with such abandon in front of a man, it never occurred to Megan to be embarrassed or self-conscious. For one thing, she was much too entranced with the pure animal grace of Holt's body to think much about how he might see her.

She reached up to touch his bare chest, which the fading daylight from her living room window cast in gorgeous relief. She would have touched him elsewhere, but he stopped her, grabbing her hand and kissing the palm and the inside of her wrist, making her shudder with anticipation. For what seemed like forever he postponed that delicious moment when their bodies would come together, skin to skin. He ran one finger up her arm, across her collarbone and down to one pouty nipple, which pebbled into a diamond-hard peak.

Their gazes collided and the fire burned white-hot. She had to fight to keep from squirming with the desperate urge she had to pull him to her and envelop him, to become part of him. But she waited, dragging out the moments of exquisite torture.

Holt groaned and covered both her breasts with his hands. He wasn't gentle, and yet he stopped short of actually causing pain. Megan threw back her head and drew in one shaky breath after another. The pleasure his touch caused her was almost too much to bear.

Just when she thought she couldn't stand it another second, he drew her to him, so that the soft, curling hair of his chest abraded her ultrasensitive nipples. The obvious evidence of his own arousal pressed against her abdomen. All she had to do was rise up on her knees. . . .

And that was exactly what Holt had in mind. He grasped her calf in one firm hand and wrapped her leg around his waist. With his other hand he supported her hips, bringing their bodies to that first joltingly intimate contact.

He pulled her downward with agonizing slowness, entering her by degrees. It was a tight fit, slightly painful at first—it had been so long for her—but the small discomfort quickly gave way to an indescribably wonderful pressure, the sensation of being filled to her limits, the ultimate intimacy of joining fully with another human being. She rejoiced in it, crying out with sheer delight.

With each eager thrust she climbed higher, transcending all known limits of sensation. Even so, her climax took her by surprise, culminating in a silent explosion that rocked her to her foundations.

She clung to him blindly, vaguely aware that he had found his own release. Afterward, they were both so still, they could have been carved from marble. The room was almost dark, illuminated only by the faint glow of city lights. The only sound, besides their breathing, was the rattling air conditioner.

Even before they were physically separated, Megan knew there were going to be problems with their indiscretion. Maybe she was crazy, but she wouldn't take it back, not for anything.

"We can't really blame this on the wine, can we?" she said weakly.

"'Fraid not, sweetheart. No one to blame but ourselves and a whole lot of hormones."

It was more than that, for her at least. But she wouldn't talk about her feelings for Holt—not yet. They were too fresh, and she wanted to explore them at leisure, by herself, before she aired them.

"Do you feel better?" he asked, sounding genuinely concerned.

"As a matter of fact, yes. Thank you."

"Please, don't thank me. I don't deserve that." He pulled away from her and began groping in the darkness for his clothes.

She didn't feel like getting dressed, so she pulled an African blanket off the back of the sofa and wrapped herself in it. "Why don't you deserve to be thanked? You helped."

"Then why don't I feel very noble about it? You were thinking about your lost love, the father of your child, and I jumped in during a weak moment."

"Trust me, I wasn't thinking about Daniel, not after you kissed me." How could she possibly hold on to thoughts of any other man while in Holt Ramsey's arms?

"I could have at least taken you into the bedroom."

She giggled at that, thinking about what a disaster *that* would have been. Her bedroom was knee-deep in debris from her whirlwind cleaning tour.

"What's so funny?"

"I'll explain it someday. You, um, sound like you're getting ready to leave."

"I think that would be best, don't you?"

Not at all, but she'd kept him here long enough. She said nothing.

"This isn't fair to Brian," he added.

Brian. He should have been at the center of her consciousness, and instead she kept holding thoughts of him at bay. "No, I guess it isn't. He'll have enough to handle without the added burden of you and me...." She sighed. "Does that mean we have to pretend this never happened?"

Holt was silent a long time before answering. "It might be best."

Damn, but she had to agree with him. "All right. But I don't regret it."

Still half-undressed, he sat back down on the sofa and took her hand. "Neither do I. You're an incredible woman, Megan."

Even as her heart soared with his words, a part of her wanted to cry. Such a tragedy, to find something so special and be unable to pursue it. "Will you tell Brian the truth tonight?" she asked. "About me being his birth mother, I mean."

"I s'pose I'll have to. No way around it. But I'm sure he'll want to talk to you about it."

Raw panic seized Megan in a painful grip. In addition to all the anger and grief she was trying to deal with, not to mention this new little wrinkle between her and Holt, she was suddenly frightened to death of dealing with Brian. What if she fell short of his expectations? What if he decided he didn't really want her in his life? There was no way she could hope to compete with Shelley, the mother he had obviously loved very much.

"I think he can handle it," Holt continued.

Megan nodded. "He seems like a pretty mature kid."

"So when do you want to get together with him?"

Panic welled up again. "I, uh, I need some time, Holt. I need to be sure I have myself together first. The last thing I want to do is to get hysterical in front of Brian. It might scar him for life or something."

Holt didn't reply for a long time. Had she said the wrong thing? Surely he wouldn't begrudge her some distance from what could only be described as emotional trauma. He was the one who had pointed out her precarious psychological state.

"Okay," he finally said. "You just call when you're ready. Meanwhile, I'll let you know if my investigator makes any progress in finding Daniel." He rose from the couch, suddenly businesslike. "You sure you'll be okay?"

"Yes, I'm fine."

"Oh, one more thing. I looked over your bid, and everything seems in order. I'll send the signed copies to your office in the morning."

Good Lord, she'd forgotten all about that infernal kitchen of his. Great. Ready or not, she would be seeing a lot of the Ramseys.

On the drive home, Holt thought about Shelley. He expected to feel remorse, or some sense of having been unfaithful, but he didn't. Before she died, Shelley had told him not to waste his life mourning. She'd wanted him to find someone else to love, someone who could be a mother to Brian.

With an ironic smile, he wondered whether Shelley had meant for him to follow her instructions so literally. Of all the women in the world, why did he have to crave the one he absolutely shouldn't have? Life wasn't fair, sometimes.

As he pulled into the garage, he turned his thoughts to more immediate concerns.

"Dad? Is that you?"

"Yeah, it's me," Holt called wearily as he came through the garage door, nearly meeting Brian in a head-on collision.

"Did you see her? Ms. Carlisle's mother, I mean." Brian's gaze darted to the mascara stain on Holt's shirt, but he made no reference to it.

"Yes, we saw her." Holt saw no point in dragging out the news. "And you were right. Megan is your birth mother."

It was rewarding to see Brian's face split into a happy grin. Holt had seen so little joy in his son's face since Shelley's death. But that unbridled delight was troubling, too. There was so much potential for disappointment.

"When can I see her?" Brian immediately asked. "Should I call her or something? Why didn't you bring her back here with you? Hey, I have a grandmother, too. What's she like? Dad? Is something wrong?"

"Nothing's wrong, really," Holt hedged. "It's just more complicated than we ever imagined." As he poured lemonade for both of them, he explained as best he could the emotion-packed meeting between Megan and her mother, and Megan's subsequent upset.

"You mean, she might not want to see me?" Brian asked, obviously fighting to keep his despair from showing.

"Oh, she will, eventually," Holt quickly assured, praying he was right. "She just needs some time to sort things out. This whole thing has been quite a shock to her."

Brian appeared anything but satisfied with that answer. "Did she say anything about my father?"

"She doesn't know where he is. But she did tell me that she once loved him." And maybe she still did. Holt had shied away from asking her that. "When they found out about you, they wanted to get married, but her parents wouldn't allow it. They really did a number on her."

"Sounds like she got a raw deal. But I'm still glad they took me away from her."

"Why's that?" Holt asked sharply, his protective instincts rearing up again. It was okay for him to doubt Megan's sincerity or her maternal instincts, but he didn't want anyone else, not even Brian, doing so.

"'Cause if they hadn't, you and Mom couldn't have adopted me."

"Oh." Hell, the kid was destined to be a diplomat. He knew exactly the right thing to say to ease Holt's insecurities.

A hug might not be cool to his teenage son, but Holt wrapped his arms around Brian anyway. Sometimes he forgot how lucky he really was.

Seven

As she pulled up to the curb in front of the Ramsey home, Megan had to admit she was more apprehensive about seeing Holt again than she was about meeting Brian in her new role as his birth mother. She had already talked to them both on the phone. Brian had seemed cautious but upbeat. Holt, on the other hand, had been cool and businesslike in making arrangements for visitation—not what she'd expected, after what they'd shared.

True to his word, Holt was setting no limits on Megan's contact with Brian, provided Brian was agreeable. But there had been an unmistakable note of warning in his voice. Although he hadn't come out and said it, Megan had gotten the distinct impression that Holt was telling her that, once she established a relationship with Brian, she'd better follow through.

Well, she supposed she couldn't blame him for his protectiveness. The kid had been through a lot. But had she given Holt any reason to suspect that she was less than sincere in her desire to know her son?

She stood on the front porch, her heart beating like a kettledrum, and rang the bell. The door opened almost immediately and Brian was standing there, welcoming her with a goofy grin. "Hi, c'mon in. Dad's not home with the tickets yet, but he'll be here soon."

Megan had sworn she wouldn't cry again, especially in front of Brian. Nonetheless, a single tear slid down her cheek as she followed him inside.

Brian. Her son. He really was her son. She still had a hard time believing it.

"You want something to drink?" he asked.

He had manners, Megan mused as she surreptitiously brushed the errant tear away. Holt had raised him well. Holt *and Shelley.* "Some water would be nice."

Brian fetched a glass from the dining room table, where the dishes were temporarily stored, then filled it with ice and water from the refrigerator, the only part of the kitchen left intact. The contractors had started ripping out cabinets that morning, and they'd obviously gone after their job with gusto. The place looked like a tornado had come through.

Megan accepted the water with a smile, wishing Holt would get home so they could all go somewhere, do something. She wasn't exactly nervous around Brian, but she would feel awkward until their relationship developed some parameters.

"What should I call you?" Brian asked suddenly.

Ah, there was one parameter. Megan pondered the question of a name as she settled into one of the frayed rattan chairs in the dining room. "'Ms. Carlisle' does seem a rather formal way to address one's mother."

Brian smiled briefly, then sobered. "I hope you understand if I don't call you 'Mom,'" he said, his voice full of apology. "But that would get kind of mixed-up, since there's already someone I call that."

"I understand completely," she replied, silently vowing that she would never let him know how it hurt. " 'Mom' isn't exactly a title I've earned. How would it be if you called me Megan?"

He thought for a moment. "But that's what everyone else calls you."

"Hmm." She took a long sip of the cool water. "Hey, I know. You could call me Meg. That's what Daniel used to call me, but no one else did."

"My real father," Brian said somberly. "I mean, my *birth* father. Dad has a fit if I use the word *real*. He always reminds me that he and Mom are my *real* parents, 'cause they raised me."

"I don't blame him. If I had raised you, I would feel just as possessive." She hadn't planned on making this speech so soon, but Brian was plainly worried about the confusion of having two mothers. "Brian, I want you to know that I have no intention of stepping in and trying to take your mother's place. I just want us to get to know each other."

He nodded.

"So what do you think? Is Meg okay?" She thought it rather appropriate.

He nodded again. "Okay, I'll try it." He stared out the window at the patio, where someone, probably Holt, had been trimming and weeding. The area looked much more well manicured than the last time she'd been here.

"Will you tell me about my fath—about Daniel?" Brian asked.

That was another question Megan had been anticipating. Daniel, the drifter, the older boy from the wrong side of the tracks whose aura of danger and defiance of authority had been irresistibly tempting to an overprotected seventeen-year-old. Lately she'd done a lot of thinking about him, wondering if she'd really loved him.

"You look a lot like him," Megan said. She was saved from further explanations by the sound of the back door opening. Her heart started hammering again, as it did every time Holt came within a hundred feet of her. Only now, she had the memory of their lovemaking to add to her distress.

Brian darted around the corner to greet his dad. Megan could hear their voices.

"Did you get the tickets?" Brian asked.

"Got 'em right here." Holt's voice was low, warm with affection. When he came around the corner into view, Megan's mouth went dry and her face flushed with heat. Every time she saw him he looked better. Even after a hot day's work he was still gorgeous, with his hair mussed and his skin bronzed another shade darker. "Hello, Megan."

"Hi," was all she could manage.

"Hurry up and get showered, Dad, so we can go. I don't want to miss the opening pitch."

"I'm not going," he said bluntly. "The guy who gave me the tickets only had two extras. Sorry. But you and Megan have a lot to catch up on, and you can probably do that better without me getting in the way."

By the tone of his voice, he wasn't sorry at all. Megan looked at him curiously, but he avoided her gaze.

Initially she'd thought it would be helpful to have Holt along during her first extended visit with Brian, to act as a buffer if needed. But maybe it would be better if she and Brian had this time to themselves. In fact, she was almost relieved that she didn't have to spend the next several hours with Holt and all that maleness, possibly sitting right next to him in those cozy seats at the Ballpark in Arlington, arms brushing, knees bumping, the scent of his after-shave teasing her nose.

Distance—that's what she needed. She had taken comfort in his arms during a vulnerable moment, and a little distance would allow those residual tugs of desire to fade.

He handed the two tickets to Brian, along with some money. "You'd better get going if you want to beat the traffic."

"Yeah, okay," Brian said, though he gave his father a perplexed look.

Holt felt an odd sensation inside his chest as he watched Megan and Brian walk out the door without him. Then he took the third ticket out of his back pocket and studied it, as if it might hold the answers he so desperately needed.

He had fully intended to go with Brian and Megan to the baseball game. But when he'd seen Megan, looking so fresh and sweet in white linen shorts and a bright purple camp shirt, he'd known he couldn't subject himself to her nearness without touching her, holding her, burying his face in her silky hair.

He must have been crazy the other night when he'd made love to her. When he'd first taken her into his arms, he'd meant only to comfort her. He would have done anything to remove that desolate look from her eyes, to take away all the hurt inflicted on her, to make her smile. But she hadn't smiled, and neither had he. She'd looked up at him with those shiny, trustful brown eyes, and somehow that first kiss had just happened.

After the kiss, he'd been lost.

Well, it wasn't going to happen again. Even if he were ready to embark on another relationship—which he wasn't—a liaison between Holt and Megan would only confuse Brian and possibly upset him. So many changes heaped on the kid all at once would be too much for him to handle.

No, the best thing would be for Holt to just stay out of the picture when Megan and Brian were together. He wouldn't do anything to jeopardize Brian's emotional well-being.

Holt threw together a submarine sandwich for dinner, but it was less than satisfying. He was craving a ball game hot dog. He took a shower, read a few pages of a bestseller without retaining any of it, watched a couple of inane programs on television. The baseball highlights on the ten o'clock news did nothing to improve his mood.

At eleven he resorted to pacing.

It was almost eleven-thirty when Brian got home. Holt found himself holding his breath when he heard the key in the door, wanting to catch a glimpse of Megan, but Brian entered the house alone.

"You missed an awesome game, Dad. Gonzales tripled in the bottom of the eighth with the bases loaded, and we came back to win seven to six."

Holt couldn't muster much enthusiasm for the Rangers' victory. "That's great," he managed. "How did the rest of it go? Did you and Megan . . . you know, get along okay?"

Brian looked at him like he'd asked a really stupid question. "Sure. She told me all about how she grew up rich and everything. She had a nanny and her own horse."

"Really? What else did you talk about? Or maybe it's none of my business," Holt added, hoping he wouldn't sound too nosy.

"She told me about my re—my biological father. He sounds like a pretty cool dude. I hope that P.I. finds him."

Holt gritted his teeth. Although he felt like a traitor to Brian, he was hoping just the opposite. He didn't want Brian's biological father to come back into their lives. Or back into Megan's.

That insidious prickling that prodded him every time he thought about Megan and Daniel together came to life again. God, he was jealous of the love those two had once shared, the love that had created Brian. Or maybe he was worried that their love would flare to life again, if they were reunited.

So what if it did? That might be the best thing that could happen. Megan would be safely out of reach then.

". . . but she didn't make any promises."

Holt realized he'd tuned out Brian's monologue. "Promises?"

"About seeing my grandmother. I thought it might be neat to have a grandma, since I never got to know mine, but Meg's mother doesn't sound like the grandma type. Meg says she's never baked a cookie in her life, and that the two of them don't get along real well, so she might not even want to meet me. Isn't that kind of weird, not wanting to meet your own grandkid? You'd think she'd be curious, at least."

"You'd think." It amused Holt to imagine Rolanda Carlisle in the role of grandmother. He wondered if she was coming to terms with the terrible thing her husband had done, or if she would ever be able to welcome Megan and Brian into her life despite Cramer Carlisle's deathbed wishes.

"I told Meg about the All-Star League. She thought it sounded neat."

"Brian, I already told you you can't join that soccer team. The All-Star League is entirely too competitive for someone your age."

"But, Dad, there's a ton of kids younger than me already on the team. One guy is only thirteen. Coach Reeves said if I want to play pro someday, the All-Star League is the way to go. Professional scouts come to their games all the time."

Holt had heard it all a thousand times. "We've already settled this," he said patiently. "If you play well in high school, you'll make a college team, and then the professional scouts can watch you all they want. Until then, your schoolwork comes first. Is that clear?"

"Okay, okay. Can't blame me for trying."

"And just because Meg gives something her stamp of approval, doesn't mean I will," Holt added irritably. "She doesn't know what she's talking about."

"She doesn't?" Brian grinned mischievously. "Does that mean I should ignore her advice about sex?"

Holt came unglued. "What the hell did she tell you about sex?"

"She said I should wait until I'm old enough to handle the consequences." Brian's smile turned smug. He knew logic was on his side.

"Yeah, well, okay, you can listen to some of Megan's advice, I guess. Wise guy," he added under his breath. "Go to bed. Don't forget to brush your teeth."

Once alone, he allowed his temper free rein. So, Megan had taken it upon herself to discuss sex with his son, was that it? Holt had agreed to give Megan unlimited contact with Brian, but that didn't give her a license to dole out parental advice. He intended to let her know that at the first opportunity.

The Ramsey kitchen was coming along nicely after only two weeks, Megan decided. Oh, it didn't look like much yet, but she could already see it taking shape in her mind's eye—those warm cherrywood cabinets, chocolate-brown marble countertops and a sharp black-and-white tiled floor to keep things bright. She had just finished conferring with the appliance man about the stove and refrigerator, but the dishwasher she would get from another source at a much better price. Holt would be pleased that she was staying under budget.

Or maybe not. He hadn't sounded too pleased last night when he'd insisted on scheduling a meeting with her before Brian got home from his first day of high school.

She couldn't help feeling all tingly at the prospect of seeing Holt again. He did things to her. But she was apprehensive, too. There'd been an ominous tone in his voice.

She heard the front door open and the sound of a measured tread in the marble-tiled entry hall. Suddenly she felt ill prepared to meet him. Her silk blouse was clinging to her on this hot, sticky day. She needed to comb her hair and powder her nose. But there was no time. The steps headed straight for the kitchen, and as Holt entered the room, his penetrating gaze caught Megan like a rabbit in a snare.

"Right on time, I see," he announced, his eyes flashing with furious blue fire.

Apprehension rose in Megan's chest. "You're not happy with the progress on the kitchen?" She glanced away nervously, focusing on a workman who was installing new frames and sills on one of the tall windows.

"This has nothing to do with the kitchen," Holt said curtly.

That left only one possibility. Her stomach sank. "Then maybe we should go somewhere more private," she said, holding on firmly to her poise. Her relationship with Brian was turning into something more wonderful than she'd ever imagined, eclipsing her pain over "losing" Danielle, and she figured she needed every ounce of strength and composure she could muster if Holt had a mind to challenge her visitation.

He nodded and led the way out of the kitchen. They picked a path among the floor tiling and Sheetrock stacked in the dining room, through the living room and finally onto the patio.

It was so peaceful out here, she thought again, even though it was hot as Hades today without a breath of wind. Not the place she would have chosen for an argument. She was going to develop a real aversion to this patio if Holt kept staging their unpleasant confrontations here.

"You've done some landscaping," she observed. "It looks nice."

"Never mind about that. Sit down. We have to talk about Brian."

She remained standing. "Is something wrong?"

"You bet there is. In case you hadn't noticed, Brian thinks you walk on water. He hangs on every word you say. I would appreciate it if you would pay attention to the sort of messages you're giving him."

Had the man lost his mind? "What in blue blazes are you talking about?"

"I've spent weeks arguing against this All-Star soccer team he wants to join. I almost had him convinced it was a bad idea. Then you come along and tell him you think it's a great opportunity for him, and the battle starts all over again. You have to be careful what you say to children. It's very easy to influence them the wrong way."

She didn't appreciate his patronizing tone one bit. Whirling away from him, she paced angrily to the fountain, which gurgled happily with clear water. She felt like sticking her head under that cool flow. Or better yet, *his* head. "So you're saying I'm a lousy influence on Brian?"

"No, I don't mean that." His tone softened slightly. "I haven't seen Brian so happy since Shelley died. I just want you to watch what you say."

"I'm very conscious of what I say to Brian," she retorted, gripping the edge of the concrete fountain to keep from turning around and popping Holt one on the chin. "The last thing I want is to cause him harm."

"I don't doubt your good intentions. But, let's face it, you don't have a lot of experience with kids."

"Maybe not," she conceded. *Twist the knife, why don't you?* "That doesn't mean I'm careless with my words or anything else. This soccer team he wants to join sounds great, at least the way he presented it to me."

"Forget the soccer team. What about sex?"

That made her turn around. "*Ex*cuse me?"

"You have no business talking to Brian about sex. That's my territory."

Ah-ha. Now she was beginning to understand his ire. "What, exactly, do you object to? Did I give bad advice?"

"No, but I would prefer that Brian get his advice from me!"

She'd had just about enough of this. "Look, Mr. Child-Rearing Expert, a kid his age will get advice about sex from any source *but* his parents. You ought to be glad he's talking to someone with a responsible outlook. When I was a teenager, I made a mistake, and I learned a painful lesson from it. I would like for my—for Brian to learn from my experience."

"Nevertheless—"

"And there are some questions you can't answer," she continued relentlessly. "Brian wanted to know about Daniel and me, and I feel he has every right to know. He asked straightforward questions, I gave straightforward answers and I intend to continue doing so. If you can't live with that, you better tell me now." And let the battle lines be drawn.

Holt shoved his thumbs into the pockets of his jeans. He remained silent for a long time, staring into space. "I can live with that, I suppose," he said grudgingly.

Megan relaxed a bit. She knew how hard this was for Holt. For two years he'd been Brian's only parent, the sole authority figure in his life. He didn't like sharing that responsibility. He also didn't like to see his son growing up so fast. That was plain.

"Now, what's so bad about this soccer team?" she asked, relieved to be off the subject of sex. She picked an orange bloom from a trumpet vine, brushing the soft petals against her cheek. "I thought it sounded great. Isn't soccer a clean, healthy sport?"

"It's not the game I disapprove of. I don't mind if Brian wants to play on the high school team. It's this All-Star League. They recruit the best high school players from all over the city, and they play against other cities. The games are very intense, the practices aren't regulated and they do a lot of traveling. Brian's not ready for something like that."

Megan nodded. She knew exactly where he was coming from. She had heard that same note of overprotectiveness in her own parents' voices. "Brian must be a very good player if this All-Star League wants him."

"He's a great player," Holt said, suddenly beaming with fatherly pride. "His middle school team had the best record in the whole district last year, and he was their star goalie."

"He'll make the high school team, then."

"Probably, but as a freshman he won't get as much playing time as he'd like."

"Would he get to play more with the All-Star League?" she asked.

"They have a team that's for age sixteen and under, so, yeah, he'd get more time on the field."

"Are you sure it's such a bad idea? I don't know Brian the way you do, but he seems like such a mature, intelligent kid. You don't think he could handle the pressure?"

"He could probably handle it," Holt said. "But I don't want him to lose sight of what's important. He has these ideas that he might go pro someday, and I don't want to encourage him.''

"Why not?"

"Why not?" he repeated incredulously. "It's an unrealistic goal—that's why not. He needs to concentrate on making good grades and getting into college.''

"Are you so sure it's unrealistic? Maybe Brian is destined to be the next Pelé. At any rate, playing soccer seems to be a crucial part of his life. At least he has a goal, and that's important. It doesn't seem fair to rein him in just when he's starting to soar.'' Megan felt a familiar lump rising in her throat. She turned away, staring into the crystal water. Dammit, not again! Did she always have to get so emotional around Holt?

"Why do I get the feeling you're talking about something other than Brian here?'' Holt asked, coming up behind Megan. He stopped short of touching her, but she could feel his breath on her neck. "Any particular reason you're so upset?''

"It's something I feel strongly about, that's all.'' She folded her arms and bowed her head, unwilling to look at him.

"Why?"

She hesitated to dredge up another chapter of her sad family history. But maybe it would help Holt understand. "All right, I confess, my feelings on this subject may be a little biased. I had a dream, once, too. I was into horses. I wanted to be a jockey, or a steeplechaser, maybe. I had a great horse, Tar, and I rode almost every day. I was involved in all kinds of shows, and I was starting to take quite a few ribbons and trophies, although my parents voiced the same concerns you're voicing now. They thought the competition was too intense, that it was taking up all my time, and that I should concentrate more on getting into a good college.''

"What happened?"

"When I was competing in the American Royal in Kansas City, Tar took a fall on one of the jumps, and I broke my arm."

"So they were right."

"No! They were dead wrong. Spills are an inevitable part of competitive horseback riding. It was bound to happen sooner or later, and it wouldn't have slowed me down much. But they overreacted." She took a deep breath. "Within a week they'd sold Tar and that was that."

She could tell, simply by the way Holt was breathing, that he didn't like being compared to her parents. "They were only doing what they thought was best for you."

"Yes, and you saw where that attitude led. My father thought he had the right to deny me the things I loved, simply because *he* believed it was in my best interest."

He moved around her, so that he could look into her face. "Surely you're not comparing my stand on Brian's soccer to your father stealing your baby."

"No, no, of course not. I'm just saying that sometimes parents don't know what's best for a child. If playing soccer is so important to Brian, I think you should reconsider, maybe compromise. Allow him to join the team on the provision that he maintain his grades. If he's really committed to it, he'll keep his end of the bargain."

Holt eyed her suspiciously. "Brian didn't put you up to this, did he?"

"Holt! Give me some credit, would you? You're the one who brought up the subject of soccer."

"So I did."

"I have only one thing to add. I was your basic dutiful daughter until Dad sold Tar out from under me. That's when things changed, when I started to rebel. My grades fell, and with so much idle time on my hands I started getting into trouble. That's when I met Daniel, their worst nightmare. In their effort to protect me, my parents lost me. It's something to think about."

"Brian would never turn against me," Holt said with absolute certainty.

"Probably not," Megan agreed. "He has more sense than I did at that age."

Megan's words were far from reassuring. Holt kept thinking about the subtle changes he'd seen in Brian—the brief flashes of temper, for instance, and the cockiness.

Holt had already made one bad decision by protecting Brian from knowledge of his mother's illness. Was he really an overprotective parent? Was Megan right?

"I'll think about it," he said gruffly. Then he surprised himself by taking Megan's hands in his. "Did you ever get another horse?"

"I wanted to, but Dad wouldn't hear of it. Later, when I was married, Darren wouldn't let me, either. I think he was afraid it would distract me from my wifely devotion to him. After the divorce, I wasn't able to afford a horse. They're expensive, you know." She sighed.

Holt was struck with the oddest urge to run out and buy Megan a horse. "Megan," he said softly.

She looked up at him, her face unreadable.

"I was way out of line a few minutes ago. I apologize."

"Apology accepted," she said in a husky voice.

Neither of them made any effort to move apart. Holt opened his mouth with some vague intention of declaring that they shouldn't be standing so close. The words never formed. His body simply wouldn't cooperate with his will. The cord of awareness that stretched between them every time they were in the same room had contracted to mere inches, pulling them closer by the second.

The world around them seemed to recede until they stood in a vacuum. The roar in Holt's ears blocked out the gurgling fountain, the birds, until all he could hear was his own breathing, and all he could see were Megan's eyes, alive with promise and forbidden desires, and her mouth, so pink and moist and just waiting to be claimed.

Would one more kiss hurt? Holt thought dazedly. He'd had every intention of staying away from her, but the wanting wasn't going to go away. He thought almost constantly of those few brief moments of ecstasy. It was hard as hell to touch the stars and then never reach for them again.

"We've got to stop doing this," she murmured just before their lips met in a heated rush.

Megan freed her hands from his and slipped them around his neck, pressing her soft breasts against his chest. He loosened the scarf that secured her hair and buried his hands in the soft strands of silk. She was so beautiful, so alive in his arms, vibrating with vitality like a captured bird.

How could he let her go? How could he continue to stay away from her?

The sound of a door slamming penetrated his consciousness. Megan broke the kiss with a panicked gasp, and they both looked toward the house. No one was there.

But someone had been there.

"Brian." Megan scarcely breathed the name.

Eight

They sprang apart like a couple of guilty teenagers.

"Maybe it wasn't Brian," Holt said unconvincingly. "Maybe it was one of the workmen."

But Megan knew he was grasping at straws. She steeled herself for what had to be said. "Regardless, we shouldn't have done what we did." She half hoped he would argue with her, but he didn't.

"We'd better go take care of the damage control," he said, starting for the patio door. Megan followed, her feet dragging. Why did healthy, mutual sexual attraction have to create so many problems?

When they stepped into the house's cool interior, they heard the TV blaring from the den and knew with certainty that Brian was home and had no doubt witnessed their passionate embrace.

"I don't suppose we can tell him you were getting something out of my eye," Megan said with a forced laugh.

Her attempt to lighten the mood fell flat.

"Brian's a little more savvy than that." Holt heaved a sigh of resignation. "I'll talk to him."

"And tell him what?"

"The truth—that what he saw was an impulsive act, that it won't be repeated and that it doesn't mean anything."

Megan felt as if her breath were being crushed out of her. How could he say it meant nothing? It meant something to her!

"You can skip out if you want," he offered.

She bristled. "It was as much my mistake as yours," she said coolly. Let him think she was as casual about the whole thing as he was. "We'll handle this together."

Holt nodded, then strode purposefully toward the den, Megan on his heels.

Brian greeted them with a sly, knowing smile. "Hi, Dad. Oh, hi, Meg, I didn't know you were here."

And pigs can fly, Megan thought.

"So, how was school?" Holt asked.

"Not too bad. My locker mate is a dork, though, and my English teacher, Mrs. Dillon, treats us like we're about six years old."

Megan smiled, listening fondly as Brian related the tribulations of algebra and gym class and being a freshman.

Holt seemed to be listening with half an ear, checking his watch every few seconds.

"You in a hurry, Dad?" Brian asked innocently.

"As a matter of fact, yeah. But before I go..." He glanced nervously at Megan. "There's something...you know, sometimes you look at something, and you think you see one thing, but really it's not what you think at all."

Brian appeared puzzled. "Like an optical illusion?"

"Well, sort of. But in this case, you really do see something, but it might not mean what you think it does." He shot another pleading look at Megan. "You can jump in any time."

Well, at least he was trying, she thought. "Don't you need to get back to work?"

Brian's gaze darted from one adult to the other, perhaps trying to read the undercurrents.

"As a matter of fact, I am late," Holt said. "But..."

Megan gestured toward the door. "Go ahead. Brian and I will talk."

She didn't have to say it twice. Holt flashed a grateful smile and bid them both a hasty goodbye.

"Chicken," she muttered under her breath as he made his escape.

When she returned her attention to Brian, he was watching her expectantly. She walked over and turned off the television. "Okay, let's not beat around the bush. That *was* you who slammed the patio door, right?"

He shrugged. "Hey, it's none of my business. I didn't mean to interrupt."

"Of course it's your business. He's your father and I'm your... and we shouldn't have done that."

"You mean you shouldn't have let me see."

"No, I mean we should have shown more self-control. It would be very irresponsible for your father and me to become involved."

"Why?"

"Why? Because it's not fair to you."

"Why not?"

"Well, because..." She struggled to make him understand, if only she understood it herself. "My role in your life is confusing enough, isn't it?"

"Not for me. I got it all figured out."

She began to pace. "Okay, look at it this way. Suppose your father and I got involved, and then we had a fight and broke it off. How would that make you feel?"

He furrowed his brow in a way that strongly resembled Holt. "I'd be sorry, I guess. But it wouldn't change the way you treat me, would it?"

"Well, no, of course not."

"So what's the problem?" He stared at her, suddenly intense. "It's been more than two years since Mom died. I don't want Dad to be alone his whole life."

The kid constantly amazed her. Although he was simplifying the situation, he was handling it far better than Megan would have expected from a fourteen-year-old. He was so pragmatic about the whole thing.

Would it really be harmful to Brian if she and Holt—no, better not to let her thoughts run in that direction. She was just rationalizing. She craved intimacy with him; she wanted to make love with him again, and again and again, but to do so might be courting disaster. She had only one chance with Brian; she wouldn't blow it.

"I don't think your father really wants me complicating his personal life," she said carefully. "He's having enough trouble dealing with my relationship to you. He's been very understanding and accommodating, and I don't want to do anything to make him regret his letting me get to know you."

"If you're afraid Dad would get mad at you and stop you from seeing me, you don't have to worry. He's not like that."

No, he wasn't, Megan silently agreed. No matter how badly things went between the two of them, Holt wouldn't stop her from spending time with Brian unless he felt the contact was somehow detrimental. He wouldn't rescind his promise to let her know her son.

"I guess it's really none of my business," Brian continued. "But I just want you to know that, if you and Dad want to be together, it won't bother me."

She wasn't quite sure how to respond to that. She finally nodded. "I'll keep that in mind."

As their conversation turned to other topics, part of Megan's mind mulled over their previous discussion. Brian had encouraged her to become romantically involved with Holt. Were his motives as unselfish as they seemed? Or was he trying, perhaps unconsciously, to re-create the family unit that had been torn apart by Shelley's death? Was he trying to replace Shelley?

The idea that she could take Shelley's place glittered invitingly in her mind before she ruthlessly squelched it. What was she thinking? She had lost the chance for a normal, happy family life when her child had been taken from her and Daniel had abandoned her. Now fate had offered her an opportunity to restore some of what she'd lost—she had a role, albeit a limited one, in Brian's life. That was enough. That had to be enough.

Holt stood in front of the security door of Megan's apartment building, his finger poised over her doorbell. As much as he wanted to see her, he was dreading this visit. He had already brought so much pain into her life.

He'd done a damn good job avoiding Megan the past few weeks, but that didn't mean he hadn't thought about her. And he had. A lot. He had never wanted a woman the way he wanted her, not even during his and Shelley's courting days. He even dreamed about Megan, about the way her skin felt, quivering beneath his touch, and the sweet, soft roundness of her breasts. Sometimes he awoke and imagined her scent still in the air.

He never should have given in to his desires that first time. But what sane man could have turned her down? Then again, who said he was sane? he thought as he pressed down on the buzzer. Here he was, returning to the scene of the crime.

He really had no choice. What he had to tell Megan required utmost privacy.

"Yes, who's there?" she asked over the intercom.

God, even her voice made him crazy. He wondered what he had interrupted that made her sound so breathless. "It's Holt Ramsey."

There was a long pause. Surely she wouldn't deny him entry. Granted, they hadn't been on the best of terms lately, but... actually, they hadn't been on any terms lately.

The security door buzzed, and he let himself in and climbed the stairs.

She opened her door before he even knocked, and the sight of her stole the breath right out of his lungs. She was wrapped in a baby blue terry robe, the hem of which hit her midthigh. Her hair was wet and she wore no makeup. Now he knew what he'd interrupted.

"I just got out of the shower," she said with a helpless shrug as she let him in. Her body emanated a clean, soapy scent.

"Are you going out?" he asked, as if it were any of his business. But it was Friday night, after all. She might have a date.

"No, I just felt hot and sticky after work."

He was definitely relieved, making him wonder what he would have done if she'd said yes. Would he have asked her whom she was seeing, then waited for the bum to show up at her door so he could rearrange his face?

This possessiveness of his was ridiculous. He had no hold on her...but she had a helluva hold on him, and she probably didn't even know it.

"Would you like something to drink? Actually, I was about to serve up some gazpacho for dinner. Have you eaten?"

"Uh, Megan, I don't need anything. Can we sit down? I have to talk to you about something important."

Her hand flew to her mouth. "Is it about Brian? He's okay, isn't he?"

"Brian's fine," he assured her as they moved toward the sofa.

The sofa, where Megan had given herself to him so sweetly, so passionately...Holt quickly veered to a basket chair, allowing Megan to have the couch to herself. She pushed a pile of work onto the floor and curled up on one end, adjusting the sparse hem of the robe to cover her thighs.

"I just came from a meeting with Benny Powell," he began.

Megan clasped her hands in her lap, forming a tight, bloodless knot with her fingers. "The P.I. He found Daniel, didn't he." It was a statement, not a question.

"Yes."

"So, what, he's married and has ten kids, right? And he doesn't even want to meet Brian. Or he's in jail."

"No, I'm afraid it's worse. He's...he's dead." Holt hated himself for blurting out the news.

Her face paled and she looked away. "You're sure?"

"Yeah. He was in a motorcycle accident more than ten years ago."

Her face contracted with pain and she lowered her head, staring down at her hands. It was all Holt could do to stop himself from going to her, holding her, absorbing some of the hurt. But he knew if he held her, he wouldn't let her go.

Megan looked up after a few moments, her lips pressed into a thin white line. "Daniel lived in the fast lane, and he always said he would die there, too. I guess he was right."

Holt had expected her to cry, but apparently she wasn't going to.

"I'm sorry to break it to you this way, Megan."

"What other way is there?" She stood suddenly. "I think I'll get a drink. Sure you don't want one?"

"No, thanks."

He left her alone, resisting the urge to follow her and make sure she was really okay, that she wasn't just putting up a strong front for his sake. If she wanted to shed a few tears in private, that was her business. But she returned after a minute or so, still dry-eyed, although her hands trembled ever so slightly.

She set a full wineglass on the coffee table in front of him. "In case you change your mind," she said, then took a sip from her own glass. "It's Chablis."

"You're taking this awfully well," he couldn't help observing.

"Am I?" She sank back onto the sofa, no longer paying much attention to the hem of her robe.

He tried not to focus on those shapely legs.

"I'm not really the hysterical type," she said, "despite what you've seen. Daniel was a part of my past, my girlhood. I've already mourned his passing, in a way."

"I thought maybe you still had feelings for him."

"Only for the boy I used to know. I think I stopped loving him the day I realized he'd really left me and he wasn't coming back. Apparently he wasn't quite ready to be a father."

Holt felt overwhelming relief, followed quickly by guilt. He hadn't yet told her everything, and he was strongly tempted not to. Would it serve any purpose to tell her more about her father's heartless manipulations?

But was it fair to let her think Daniel had left her because he didn't care? If he told her the rest, would it resurrect her love?

"Daniel had a reason for leaving, Megan, and I don't think it was because he didn't care about you or the baby."

She stared at him, frowning. "How would you know?"

"Benny talked to Daniel's father, Bill Turner. Did you know he was a bail jumper?"

"I knew there'd been some trouble in California, and he and Daniel had left in kind of a hurry, but I never delved too deeply into just what that trouble was. I didn't want to know."

"Bill was into gambling—big time. He skipped out on a twenty-five-thousand-dollar bond in L.A. Your father knew about it."

"My fa—" Her eyes grew wide. "Oh, no."

Holt continued relentlessly, determined to get it all out in the open. "While you were in Oklahoma, your father paid a visit to the Turners. He told them if they would leave the state, and if Daniel stayed away from you, he wouldn't blow the whistle on Bill. Daniel left you to keep his father out of jail."

Megan closed her eyes against the pain. "I should have known. I keep trying to tell myself that Dad did what he thought was best for me, but—"

"Megan, not even the kindest, most forgiving soul could justify what he did to you. Anyway..." Holt had to force himself to say his next words. "Daniel loved you 'til the day he died. Bill Turner has a box of letters his son wrote you but never mailed. He said he'll send them to you, if you want." There—he'd told her everything. Now his conscience would be clear—about that, anyway.

"I'd like to read them sometime," she said. Then she surprised him with a bittersweet smile. "I can't believe it. All this time I thought Daniel had betrayed me, and really he was just protecting his father from my father. That's sort of noble, don't you think? Now we can tell Brian his biological father was a noble person."

Holt realized he hadn't even thought about telling Brian. He'd been too worried about how Megan would react. "I hope he takes the news as well as you. You *are* okay, aren't you?"

"I think so. Maybe it'll hit me later, I don't know, but right now I'm okay with it. Now that I know what happened, I feel a…a sense of closure, if that makes sense." She reached out and laid her hand on his forearm. "Thank you, Holt. Thank you for settling this for me, and for caring enough to worry how I would handle it."

He jerked away from her as if her hand were a red-hot branding iron. "Don't thank me." He stood abruptly and strode to her balcony doors, which were open to let in a breeze from the first cool front of the season. The smell of impending rain was heavy in the air.

"Why shouldn't I?"

"Because I'm a jerk, that's why. You want to know how concerned I was for your welfare? I was hoping Benny wouldn't find Daniel. And when Benny told me Daniel had died, I was relieved. No, God help me, I was ecstatic. Not that Daniel was dead, but that he wouldn't be coming into our lives." He leaned one forearm against the doorframe and stared through the screen at the wind playing tag in the trees.

It took him a moment to realize that Megan had joined him. The wind flapped at the edge of her robe, revealing for half a second one creamy thigh and the pink lace edge of her panties.

"I think what you're feeling is perfectly natural," she said. "We've both seen how easily Brian welcomed me into his life. He probably would have been just as open with Daniel, and of course that would make you uncomfortable. No one wants to believe they can be replaced. But trust me, no one could replace you in Brian's eyes. You're his father, his *real* father. Just like I can't replace Shelley."

"No?" The single, sharp syllable crackled between them.

"No," she repeated, with so much conviction that he was ashamed he'd even raised the question.

"Well, you got part of it right," he said. "I guess I was feeling a little insecure about someone replacing me. I've felt that way ever since Brian expressed an interest in finding his birth parents. But that's not all. I was glad to find out Daniel wouldn't be coming back into *your* life."

"Because he hurt me?"

"Because I was jealous of him." Holt couldn't believe he was admitting this to her.

"Jealous because Daniel and I conceived Brian?"

"No, dammit, because you were in love with him! And I was afraid that if he came back, you'd take up where you left off. And I don't know how I would have handled that."

She said nothing. She just kept staring quizzically at him with those guileless brown eyes. Ah, hell, did he have to spell it out? He was doing a lousy job with words, but there was one message she couldn't fail to understand. One step toward her, and he had her pinned against the doorframe. Her mouth still formed an "O" of surprise when he joined it to his.

She gave only token resistance before surrendering her body against his. The faint taste of Chablis lingered on her lips and tongue. Somewhere close by, wind chimes tinkled mournfully.

Holt knew he should stop, pull away, leave her. But he couldn't do it. His dreams were a poor substitute for the flesh-and-blood woman in his arms. Her kiss was, at that moment, more essential than the breath in his lungs.

If Megan had reservations, she apparently wasn't heeding them. Her mouth was as greedy as his, her hands just as restless. As she pressed her body against his, the front of her robe worked itself open, revealing the lush swell of one breast. Unable to resist temptation, he dipped his head and nuzzled the soft blue terry cloth away from his prize, then took her nipple into his mouth.

"Ah, um..." came Megan's ineloquent response. Her breathing was quick and shallow.

The first fat raindrops began to splat against the stone-tiled balcony. The wind had picked up, blowing a damp mist through the screen. Holt could taste the cool moisture on her skin as he kissed a trail from one breast to the other, felt it settling in his hair. But it did nothing to dampen their passion.

"Holt... please."

He could hear the sheer effort it had taken to dredge up her objection. He stopped and lifted his head, seeing the torture in her eyes, torture in the form of desire mixed with fear. He wouldn't have thought anything could cool his ardor, but her eyes did. "Did you want me to stop?"

"No, but... is this going to be another hit-and-run maneuver?"

She didn't have to explain further; he knew exactly what she meant. After they'd made love the first time, he'd practically run out the front door in his effort to distance himself from her. And when he'd kissed her on his patio, he'd proceeded to tell her it didn't mean anything, and that it wouldn't happen again.

He'd been a liar as well as an unthinking clod. It was a miracle she'd let him get this close again.

"If I could, I'd spend the night with you," he said, knowing that was little consolation for the way he'd treated her.

"I'm not asking that. I understand you can't because of Brian," she said. "All I'm asking—"

"—is that I don't jump up and run like your apartment is full of poisonous snakes?"

"Something like that."

"I won't." He cupped her cheek in his hand, sliding his fingers through her damp hair. "I promise, I won't run scared again. If you let me through your bedroom door, we are officially *involved*. No more trying to deny it. If that's what you want." He searched her eyes as he waited for her reply.

She stepped away from him to close the balcony doors, saving her hardwood floors from a thorough drenching. When she looked back, he plainly saw the answer he'd hoped for.

"Bedroom's down the hall, past the kitchen," she said coolly, nodding her head. Then she flashed an impish smile. "And tonight, we might even be able to find the bed once we get there."

Nine

Holt didn't understand Megan's private joke, but at the moment he didn't care to decipher it. He whisked her up in his arms—Lord, she hardly weighed more than a cat—and headed toward the room in question, all doubts forgotten.

Although it was gloomy outside, there was still enough daylight coming in through two windows that Holt could clearly see Megan's bedroom, and it was as quirky as the rest of her apartment, a mixture of Victorian romance and modern pop culture. A nineteenth-century armoire sat next to a set of Andy Warhol-like prints on the lavender walls; colorful rag rugs surrounded the geometric Art Deco bed, which was covered with a chenille bedspread in vivid pink. An antique wicker baby buggy housed a collection of vintage hats.

He took in only a few of the details as he set her down on the bed, thinking what a lot he had to learn about Megan Carlisle. Hats? Did she ever wear them?

And then his eyes were only for her. He untied the belt to her robe as she watched solemnly, then pushed the robe off her shoulders and down her arms so that it pooled around her hips.

Her skin was so soft, he thought as he ran his fingers down her bare arms, raising goose bumps. Comparing it to satin or porcelain didn't do it justice; it had a texture all its own.

She gave a small sigh of pleasure, so he stroked her arms again. The first time they'd made love had been so frantic, he hadn't had time to really appreciate the subtleties of Megan's beauty—the delicate freckles that peppered her shoulders, the neat indentation that was her navel and the way she demurely crossed her legs, as if she were sitting down for tea with the queen instead of sitting all but naked before a man who wanted to ravish her.

And her eyes. He had noticed her eyes many times, of course. Who could miss them? But he'd never watched them as she observed him undress. He saw all kinds of things in their velvet brown depths, which were anything but mild. Spurred by that inner fire he knew was burning inside her, he peeled off his clothes in record time.

"In case I've never told you, I enjoy watching you," she said, her voice even huskier than usual. "I like the way you move."

Her comment pleased him. He wanted her to think him handsome and virile. He eased her down onto the bed, swinging her legs up onto the mattress. She scooted over, making room for him. "You're pretty easy on the eyes yourself." He ran his hand from her thigh to her hip to her breast. "No, it's more than that," he said, suddenly serious. "You're beautiful. Truly beautiful inside and out."

"Thank you." Her voice was thick with emotion. "No one's ever said that to me before, not in quite that way."

"They should have." Her father should have, and Daniel, and that fink of an ex-husband of hers, Darren What's-His-Name. But Holt's brief spurt of anger quickly dissipated as he pushed those other men from his mind. Megan was his now and he would make up for all the injustices life had dealt her. He kissed her—a kiss of possession.

He had every intention of taking things slowly, savoring these precious moments, stretching out all that luscious anticipation. But his hormones had other ideas. The moment she started responding to his kiss, his body was primed for action, like a powder keg awaiting a match.

Thankfully Megan's impatience matched his, maybe even exceeded it. With no coaxing from him she removed her panties, the last barrier between them. He would forever remember the image of delicate pink lace sliding along her slender legs.

"Come inside," she whispered urgently between fevered kisses. "I want you inside."

He needed no further urging. He levered himself over her, settling into the sweet cradle between her legs, and slid his length into her warm depths.

They fit together so perfectly, he caught himself thinking. And then he didn't think at all, losing himself to the experience as his entire being centered on their union. He tried to keep his thrusts gentle; Megan was such a little thing, and she felt so fragile beneath his suddenly massive-seeming body. But she didn't want gentle, if her actions were any indication. She grasped his buttocks and pulled him against her, tilting her hips to meet his thrust, filling herself with him.

He knew when she was almost to the peak of pleasure; she closed her eyes and her heart beat faster, and she made a faint mewling noise in the back of her throat. Somehow he managed to postpone his own climax long enough to appreciate the full spectrum of Megan in the throes of passion, purely wild, uncontrolled, *beautiful*. Her muscles tightened convulsively around him in wave after exquisite wave, until his control was spent and he followed in her path.

A few minutes later, he noticed that the rain had already let up. He got up to open a window and let in some fresh air. Megan was watching him anxiously. She didn't trust him not to leave, he realized. He couldn't blame her. He would have to earn her trust.

He settled back down on the bed and drew her against him, pillowing her head against his shoulder, stroking her wildly disarrayed hair.

"Do you want me to tell Brian about Daniel?" she asked, breaking the silence.

Oddly enough, the fact that she'd mentioned Daniel so soon after making love with him didn't revive his jealousy. Tonight she had laid those feelings to rest. "I think he would accept it better coming from you. I've realized lately that I'm the pits when it comes to breaking unsettling news. I can't seem to do anything but just blurt it out. But if it's uncomfortable for you—"

"No, I don't mind. I think if he sees that I've accepted Daniel's death, he will, too. I'm more worried about what to tell Brian about us."

"No need to tell him anything. He'll know. As a matter of fact, I'm not so sure he didn't know after the first time. He eyed that mascara stain on my shirt with a real speculative gleam in his eye, but he never asked about it."

"Are you okay with that?"

"If I honestly thought we were hurting Brian, I wouldn't have let it go this far...not twice, anyway. But after talking to him about that kiss he saw—"

"Oh, so you did talk to him. That's a bone I've been meaning to pick with you. Thanks a heap for leaving me holding the bag, you big chicken."

"I admit it, I'm a subhuman coward. But I couldn't look my kid in the eye and tell him the kiss meant nothing, or that it wouldn't happen again."

"What exactly did you say?"

"That I wasn't sure how it had happened, what it meant or where it would lead. But he was very quick to assure me that he was okay with us dating."

"He said the same thing to me." She rubbed her palm over his chest, then idly swirled little circles with the tip of her finger. "I'm still worried. We've just begun, and relationships—" She rolled the word experimentally on her tongue, then shot it out in harsh syllables, as if afraid to utter it aloud. "—can have a strange effect, not only on the ones involved, but the people around them."

Holt didn't want to think about this. He'd already justified becoming involved with Megan. He didn't need a whole new set of doubts creeping in.

"I guess I shouldn't be looking for trouble," she continued. "In fact..." She turned onto her side and propped her head on her hand so she could look at him. "I know I can never replace Shelley, in your heart or Brian's. But maybe— no, never mind."

"What?" His senses were suddenly alert to a new note he heard in Megan's voice.

"Well, maybe all three of us can benefit from the way things are turning out. You and Brian will have a feminine influence in your lives, and I'll have a little taste of the family life that was taken away." She eased her head back down on his shoulder, apparently satisfied with her conclusion.

But Holt's mind had balked at the word *family*. Brian was almost too eager to see his birth mother and adopted father romantically involved. In fact, he'd made several broad hints even before he'd known who Megan was. Was it possible the boy had ideas about putting his broken family back together?

Even more disturbing, had Megan confused gratitude, comfort and yearning for a family with her feelings for Holt? If not for Brian, would Megan have allowed Holt to share her bed?

Holt's involvement with Megan was one thing; when it came to that, he'd made peace with himself and Shelley's memory. But their relationship was completely separate and independent from Brian, and marriage was out of the question. If either Brian or Megan had a new family unit in mind, they were destined for disappointment.

Brian was a truly amazing kid, Megan mused as she sat in the bleachers at a North Dallas soccer field one blustery October evening. He hadn't taken the news of Daniel's death quite as well as she'd hoped. In fact, he'd been pretty melancholy for a couple of weeks afterward. But today, when she'd picked him up to take him to the game, he seemed to have come to terms with the loss.

"I guess it's better this way," he'd said pragmatically. "Daniel might not have liked me. Or he and Dad might not have gotten along, and that would have been hard."

"Daniel would have been crazy about you," Megan argued. But she couldn't deny that Holt would have been uncomfortable if Daniel had reappeared—he'd admitted it. Sometimes Brian's perceptions were uncannily accurate.

Now, as she sat in the bleachers waiting for the game to begin, she divided her concentration between the playing field and the ticket gate. Where was Holt? He might have been held up at work, as it often happened, but surely he could break away in time to witness Brian's first start as goalie for the Dallas Sparks.

She was glad Holt had relented and allowed Brian to play for the nonscholastic team. Father and son had reached an agreement that Brian could play as long as he kept his grades up. So far, grades hadn't been a problem, and his participation with the Sparks seemed to be good for him. He was developing more confidence and poise by the day, and the fact that he was a starter said a lot for his abilities.

A referee put the black-and-white ball into play, and Megan was immediately absorbed by the action. She'd never watched much soccer before and was amazed at how fast the players moved.

A boy from the opposing team kicked the ball, sending it rocketing toward the Sparks' goal—and Brian. Brian made a flying leap for it, and Megan held her breath as he dived headfirst into the ground. He came up with the ball, a triumphant smile shining from a muddy face.

For the first time, Megan saw the intensity that worried Holt. She had thought soccer was mild compared to football. But though there weren't as many head-on collisions and body pileups, there wasn't as much protective gear, either. After the first fifteen minutes of play, plenty of the boys sported scraped knees and bruises, too, no doubt. And the way they bounced that ball off their heads...!

Megan was momentarily distracted by a diminutive woman in a floppy hat, her hair obscured by a scarf, making her way up the visitors' bleachers. The figure looked familiar, and it took Megan a few moments to realize the woman, wearing a stylish denim jumpsuit and red leather boots, could easily have passed for her mother.

Megan squinted, but she was too far away to see the face clearly. Of course, it couldn't be her mother, Megan reasoned. She couldn't imagine Rolanda attending a soccer game, certainly not to cheer for the visiting team—and *never* in that hat.

Still, thoughts of Rolanda produced a little stab of guilt. The past couple of weeks had been like a wonderful dream for Megan. She was getting to know her son, she had reestablished a friendship with Heather Shipman and she'd been glorying in Holt's romantic attentions, not to mention his fantastic lovemaking. She'd been so happy, she hadn't spared even a thought for her mother.

What was she going through right now, if anything? Holt had been right; Megan had been pretty hard on her mother. But Rolanda had made no attempt to contact Megan. Didn't that say something? She probably didn't want to be bothered by her renegade daughter and a teenage grandson.

But now, Megan couldn't help but recall the look of absolute desolation on Rolanda's face when she'd witnessed the evidence of her husband's despicable act. It must have hurt to discover that someone she idolized was capable of such selfish, hurtful manipulations.

Of course it did. Megan knew firsthand.

But she preferred to think of Rolanda as having pushed the incident aside, like it had never happened. That was her usual way of dealing with things that made her uncomfortable.

Brian had asked more than once about the grandparents he'd never met, especially his grandmother. Unlike Bill Turner, Rolanda lived here in town, and it was hard to explain to Brian why they shouldn't meet.

Megan decided she would call her mother and see if she couldn't arrange something, even if it was just a brief introduction. She owed Brian the effort.

On the field, Brian made another diving save—pretty dramatic for his first big game, she thought with a swell of maternal pride.

"Way to go, Bri!" a familiar voice behind her called out.

Utterly surprised, she looked over her shoulder to see Holt sitting several rows above her with a group of people she presumed were other parents. His gaze was fixed on the playing field, and he didn't see her.

When had he sneaked in, and how had she missed him? she thought, irritated. Hadn't he even looked for her when he arrived?

Well, at least he was here, she thought as she grabbed her purse and began climbing the bleachers. She looked forward to sitting next to his big, warm body, maybe tucking her cold hands into his. The wind was unseasonably chilly tonight.

When Holt caught sight of her, he didn't flash that welcoming smile she was coming to love. Instead, his expression was guarded. "Hello, Megan," he said, making no move to clear a place for her to sit down next to him.

The other parents sitting around him—a young couple with a baby, an older couple and a lone gentleman sporting a handlebar mustache—eyed her curiously.

"Well, Ramsey, are you going to introduce us?" the mustached man asked.

"Oh, sorry," Holt said, quickly recovering his manners—but not quickly enough to suit Megan. "This is Megan Carlisle. Megan, these are the Brewers, John and Eloise..." He rattled off the rest of the names.

Megan murmured a greeting to each, barely registering their replies. She was still marveling over Holt's behavior. He was uncomfortable. No, he was downright embarrassed. He wasn't going to admit that she was Brian's mother, or that the two of them were involved.

"Brian's playing awfully well," she said, since he'd given her no other opening.

Holt smiled, but not at her. "Yeah, he's not bad."

"Shelley was an ice skater, wasn't she?" the older woman asked. "Maybe Brian inherited her athletic ability."

Holt nodded noncommittally. He didn't correct the woman's assumption.

Megan realized these people had no idea Brian was adopted, much less that his birth mother had returned to reclaim a place in his life. Even as she registered the hurt and outrage, she knew it wasn't her place to enlighten them. She was wary of doing anything that might embarrass Brian.

"Have a seat, Megan," the mustached man—Clark, she thought his name was—invited.

"No, I just came up to say hi," she replied, knowing her voice sounded too shrill to be sincere. She turned and fled to her original seat at the bottom of the bleachers. Throughout the rest of the first half, she resisted turning to look at Holt, although she fancied she could feel his gaze burning a hole in the back of her head.

By halftime, the Sparks had a comfortable five-to-one lead over their opponents. Although Megan had brought Brian to the game, Holt was to take him home, so there was no need for her to stay. Brian was so intent on his playing, he probably wouldn't miss her. As soon as the second half started, she stood and headed toward the parking lot. She spared one over-the-shoulder look at Holt, and their gazes collided briefly. He obviously had been watching her, but he made no move to stop her departure.

During the past few weeks, Holt had proved himself the most generous of lovers. He brought her flowers and small gifts, took her out for romantic dinners and complimented her constantly. Because of Brian, they didn't flaunt their intimacy, so they weren't able to make love as often as

Megan would have liked, but when they were able to steal a few hours alone, they dropped into a sensual world unlike anything she'd ever experienced. He satisfied her body and soul, giving of himself so completely that it often brought her to tears.

She had known for quite some time that she loved him, and that love grew day by day. Lately she'd begun to entertain those first tender realizations that he might love her back, or at least that the potential was there.

It had never occurred to her that Holt might be ashamed of her! Just now he certainly hadn't acted like a man in love. His attitude cut her deeply.

She was so lost in her thoughts, it was a while before she heard the crunch of footsteps several feet behind her in the gravel parking lot. She resisted the urge to turn and look. The parking lot was deserted and dark. What if there was a mugger following her?

Or maybe it was Holt, she thought with a grain of hope. He would apologize for his treatment of her, invite her to join him and his friends. As she neared her Jeep, she took her keys out of her purse, bunched them into her fist, then whirled around rapidly, ready for anything.

The last person she'd expected to see was the woman in the floppy hat. "Mother?"

"Hello, Megan."

"What are you doing here? And in disguise, for heaven's sake?"

"I followed you here. I've been following you around for the past few days, as a matter of fact. I knew sooner or later you'd visit with Brian."

"Mother, you're kidding!" Megan was so flabbergasted at the thought of her mother sneaking around in disguises that it took a moment for her to understand the implications. "You wanted to see Brian?"

"I wanted to see him, but I didn't want him to see me."

Megan crossed her arms and leaned back against the vehicle. "Idle curiosity, or what?"

A gust of wind tugged at the brim of Rolanda's hat, and she shivered. "My car is just down the row. Would you... can I buy you some coffee?"

The vulnerability in her mother's voice touched Megan as nothing else could have. Rolanda had always been so confident, so sure of herself, at least when it came to dealing with her daughter. "All right," Megan agreed cautiously.

As they climbed into the brand-new silver Mercedes, Megan realized she'd seen the car in her apartment's parking lot more than once and had wondered how anyone in her building could afford such an extravagance.

Rolanda drove cautiously, like someone who wasn't accustomed to being behind the wheel. She seldom was. Her preferred mode of transportation was chauffeured limo. They parked at a diner a few blocks away from the soccer field.

"So, what do you think of your grandson?" Megan asked as soon as they were seated with steaming coffee in front of them.

"I think he's a fine, handsome boy. I see a little of my brother in him, your uncle Rick. But mostly he looks like Daniel. Have you found Daniel yet?"

"He died several years ago," Megan related in an emotionless voice.

"Oh, Megan, I'm sorry."

"Are you?" Some of the old hurt resurfaced. "You certainly never much cared for him when he was alive."

"I worried that he was too old for you, too... I don't know, too adult, I guess. I saw the looks that passed between you, and I knew what was going on. But I never really thought he was a bad person, and he was certainly handsome as the devil. I was surprised by the way he just up and left.''

"You were?"

"Why, yes. When the two of you told us you were pregnant, he seemed so sincere about wanting to marry you.''

Megan saw no point in telling her the true reason Daniel had deserted her. She would let her mother hold on to whatever illusions she might have about her husband's integrity.

"Speaking of handsome as the devil,'' Rolanda continued, "why weren't you sitting with Mr. Ramsey?"

"He didn't want to sit with me. Apparently he's embarrassed by my relationship to Brian. His friends don't even know Brian is adopted." The admission brought a burning to Megan's eyes, but she blinked back the impending tears.

"Oh, honestly, men and their pride! They can be so stupid and hurtful! You're good enough to share his bed, I noticed, but he can't even acknowledge you to his friends?"

"Mother!" Megan was mortified. She'd never heard such frank words from Rolanda.

"I'm sorry to speak so plainly, dear, but the fact is I *have* been watching you for the past few days, and your relationship to Holt is pretty evident." Oddly enough, there was no disapproval in her voice.

"Holt is a good man," Megan said, amazed that she would come to his defense so quickly. "I'll be forever grateful to him for the way he's raised Brian. He's allowed me unlimited visitation, you know."

"So he's a good father," Rolanda agreed. "Does that mean he's the right man for you?"

The question gave Megan pause. Holt had given her something very precious in reuniting her with her son. Was it possible she was confusing her gratitude with other, deeper feelings?

"I don't know," she finally answered. His treatment of her tonight had certainly given her reason to doubt his feelings, if not hers.

"How is Brian handling your sudden reappearance?" Rolanda asked.

Megan smiled. "Wonderfully. He's the most open-minded, accepting child you can imagine. He's given me nothing but joy. He asks a lot of questions about you, too."

Rolanda reared back in surprise. "Me?"

"It's only natural he should want to learn about his grandparents." Megan looked at her watch. "The game's not over yet. We could go back, and you could meet him."

Rolanda shook her head vehemently. "Oh, I couldn't."

"Why not?"

"Well, it's just not seemly, springing something like that on the child when he's not expecting it. Another time, perhaps."

The glow of warmth Megan had started to feel for her mother faded abruptly. She was curious about Brian, but nowhere near ready to risk a relationship with him.

"It's getting late," Megan said curtly as she slapped some money on the table and slid out of the booth. Sometime when she wasn't quite so irritated she would hold her mother to that *another time, perhaps.*

The door buzzer awoke Megan from a light, restless sleep. She squinted at her bedside clock and saw that it was after midnight. What in the world...?

She threw on a long white cotton robe—too light for this chilly weather—and stumbled to the intercom.

"Who's there? And this better be good."

"It's Holt," came the weary voice. "I need to talk to you."

"Yeah? Well, I don't want to talk to you," she shot back peevishly. "It's the middle of the flippin' night, Ramsey. Why don't you try me at a more civilized hour? Or are you afraid someone might see you associating with me?"

"Megan, please. Let me at least try to explain."

She knew she should send him home. If she let him come up here, the scene of most of their romantic trysts, she would find it much more difficult to stay angry at him. And she needed to stay angry.

"I'll come down," she said curtly. She wrapped her robe more tightly around her and tied the belt in a knot—as if that could protect her from his potent masculinity—and headed downstairs, not even bothering to find her slippers.

She regretted that decision as her bare feet hit the cold tile floor of the entry foyer. She really regretted not dressing more substantially when she saw Holt, overpowering the delicate Queen Anne chair in which he sat. Endearingly rumpled, properly penitent, he looked right at her with those sincere blue-gray eyes, and the thin robe might as well have been made of cobwebs for all the protection it gave her.

Resolute, she sat in the chair farthest from him, crossing both her arms and her legs. "Okay, let's hear it."

"You've met Brian's friend Peter Brewer, haven't you?" he began.

Megan nodded. "He plays for the Sparks, too."

"The younger couple I was sitting with are Peter's parents. They were good friends when Shelley was ill. I can't tell you how many times I dumped poor Brian on them with no notice when I needed an emergency sitter. And when Shelley died, they stood by me. When other friends drifted away, John and Eloise were there, shoring me up, forcing me to go on when I felt like quitting."

"It's good that you had such friends," Megan commented blandly, wondering what exactly this had to do with her.

"I guess I wasn't expecting to see them at the game," he continued. "When you showed up, I felt so damned awkward, I didn't know what to do. How do I introduce you? John and Eloise know Brian's adopted, but Eloise's parents—the older couple sitting with us—didn't know. It's an extremely complicated situation, and not one I care to explain casually in the bleachers at a soccer game."

"I appreciate how awkward the situation was. But I don't want my relationship with Brian hidden like dirty linen in a cupboard, or spoken of in hushed tones. I've done nothing wrong, and I don't want Brian to take a cue from you and believe he should be ashamed of me."

"That would never happen. But you're right. Just because I'm uncomfortable doesn't excuse the way I behaved toward you."

She wasn't quite ready to forgive. "You could have at least smiled. You greeted me less warmly than you would have the check-out lady at the grocery store."

"I'm sorry, Megan. I know I acted badly. If I'd had a chance to think it through..."

"What would you have done differently?"

"I would have introduced you as a friend, at least, and asked you to sit down."

That wasn't exactly the answer Megan had been looking for. "Not your girlfriend?" she asked, arching one eyebrow.

Holt thought before he answered. "That probably would have been the thing to do, I guess."

"Your enthusiasm is overwhelming."

"Megan, please, try to understand. To the Brewers I've been the grieving husband for more than two years. To suddenly change roles and admit that I've found someone new..."

Damn, she understood all too well. "You're embarrassed by me."

"I wouldn't put it that way."

"Whatever delicate terms you couch it in, if you can't admit to dear friends that you're seeing me, you're obviously not ready for a relationship."

"Megan, be reasonable—"

She stood abruptly. "When you're ready to admit to the world that we're a couple, maybe we'll have a chance. Until then, I won't be your part-time lover, hanging around when it's convenient, magically disappearing when it's not."

She turned and tried to open the security door, belatedly realizing she'd locked herself out. So much for her dramatic exit.

"It's just as well you can't leave yet," he said to her back. "Because I have something else to say. Maybe I do have some things to work out. But we swore, both of us, that nothing between us would hurt Brian. I want you to keep that promise."

"Why do you think I wouldn't?"

"You didn't stay to watch him win his first soccer game. When it was over, he wondered where you were. I lied and said you left because you weren't feeling well. I don't like being put in that position." He opened the security door with the key she'd given him.

Megan snatched the key out of his hand as outrage bubbled up inside her. "If you don't like lying, you should have told him the truth—that you were so *rude,* you drove me away!" With that she slid through the door and raced up the stairs, afraid to look back.

Ten

Holt's kitchen was a disaster area. The remodeling had been going on for seven weeks now, when it was supposed to have been completed in six. He was tired of tripping over the pile of molding that had been ripped out, refinished and now awaited installation. He was tired of the trucks that rolled over his shrubs. He was tired of the noise and the fine sheen of dust that covered everything in the house.

Most of all he was tired of having no one to complain to. Ever since their midnight altercation in the foyer of her apartment building, Megan had proved to be slippery as a bar of soap. She was never in her office, she avoided running into him at the house, and when she did return phone calls, she always managed to do it when he didn't have the time to air his grievances.

He'd left work early today because of a pounding headache, only to realize that his home was no refuge. The workers' hammers and power tools—not to mention their penchant for loud country-and-western music—wasn't doing his head any good. He'd been just about to retreat to his car and drive somewhere—anywhere—when he'd spotted a familiar Jeep pulling up to the curb.

Aha, now he had her. He could show her firsthand the wreck her subcontractors had made of his house and demand that she do something about it.

Through a front window he watched her climb out of the Jeep, wearing a fuzzy sweater dress the color of orange sherbet, her hair tied loosely with a satin ribbon the same color. A gust of wind molded the dress against her body, and for a moment all Holt could think about was touching her. The remembered softness of her breasts and firmness of her legs wrapped around him brought a tightness to his chest— and elsewhere.

Damn, but the woman had a way about her. Something inside him spun out of control whenever she was around. But control was something he needed if he wanted to deal with her successfully, to say what he had to say. He squared his shoulders and met her at the front door.

"Oh! Holt, I didn't know you were home."

"Obviously, or you wouldn't be here. You've done a good job avoiding me."

"I haven't deliberately avoided you," she said indignantly as he closed the door behind her. "It's just that I've been so busy. One of our designers quit unexpectedly, and I got several of his jobs dumped in my lap." She ruffled her bangs with one nervous hand and avoided his gaze. "Anyway, I didn't think you'd be too eager to see me."

"Well, you're wrong there. When is this kitchen from hell going to be finished, anyway? You're already running a week later than you promised."

For a moment she appeared surprised at his acid tone. A flash of pain showed in her velvet eyes. But professionalism quickly took a front seat. "Six weeks was an estimate. Some things, like those custom cherry cabinets, have taken longer than expected. You ought to know how these jobs work sometimes. I'm sure some of your landscaping contracts run over."

She had him there.

"Besides," she continued, "we're closer than you think. All that's left are your appliances—"

"And the cabinet doors and half the countertop. And what's that pile of trim in the dining room?"

"Is that still there?"

"Yes, it's still there, along with my old stove, a stack of plumbing pipes and someone's old work boots!"

She chewed on her lower lip. "I'm sorry. You have every right to be angry. Those things should have been cleared out a long time ago. If you'll let me borrow your phone, I'll make sure the mess is cleaned up this afternoon. Are there any more problems?"

Hell, yes, there's a problem! She was treating him like just another customer, like they'd never shared anything more intimate than choosing paint colors. But then, less than a week ago he'd been guilty of the very same thing.

She looked up at him with those doe eyes, eyes that were shielded, showing no emotion.

"No, that's all," he said, pressing his fingertips to his temples. "Unless you can stop that infernal hammering."

"The faster they hammer, the faster the job gets done. But I might convince the workers to turn down their radio." She turned toward the kitchen just as every light in the house blinked off and some twangy country-and-western singer's voice went blessedly silent. A series of curses in English and Spanish issued from the kitchen.

"Now what?" Megan muttered on a frustrated sigh.

Holt felt a twinge of guilt. He was frustrated, too, although it had little to do with the kitchen. Complaining about the mess was the easiest way to target the source of his aggravation.

Apparently Megan had been serious when she'd told him their relationship was finished. She was convinced he wasn't yet over Shelley's death, that he wasn't ready to fully accept another woman in his life. He was ready, dammit. But that didn't mean they wouldn't hit a little bump now and again.

All right, so he'd handled things badly at the soccer game. He would do better next time. What did she want him to do, throw a party and make an announcement that he and Megan were sleeping together? Take out an ad in the paper?

Short of such drastic action, how could he convince her that they could work things out?

Megan returned from the kitchen to find Holt still standing where she'd left him in the dim entryway, his brow furrowed in thought. "I called the electric company," she said. "Apparently some road construction caused the power failure. Lights are out all over the neighborhood, and they won't be restored for a couple of hours. I told the workers they could go home as soon as they cleaned up the mess in the dining room. They'll set the appliances by the curb, and someone will pick them up tomorrow morning. Is that all right?"

"That's fine," he said distractedly.

"Was there something else?"

"Yes. Megan, we need to talk. I know you're busy, but if you could spare a few minutes..."

She looked at her watch, wishing desperately that she had a pressing appointment to make. But her next one was more than an hour away. She wasn't sure she was ready for whatever Holt wanted to say, but she was stuck. "I have some time," she said. "Should we go out onto the patio?" At least they would be able to see each other.

"We haven't had much luck on the patio," he said, managing a wry smile. "How about the living room?"

"Okay." She preceded him into the huge formal living room, which was oddly intimate with the drapes closed and the lights off. There was just enough illumination that Megan could see her way to one of the old wingback chairs.

Rather than sitting down, Holt paced nervously. "I'm not happy with the way we left things between us."

Megan made no reply at first. He'd hardly given her an apology, which was what her pride demanded. But her heart demanded that she come to an understanding with Holt. "I'm not happy, either," she finally said. "I shouldn't have lost my temper."

"You were right to be angry. I shouldn't have been so worried about what John and Eloise would think of you."

"They're your friends. It's only natural for you to be concerned with what they think." She crossed her arms. "But what I think is important, too."

"I know that. I wouldn't purposely hurt you for the world. And I should have known that the Brewers would understand completely, because they are my friends. And they want to be yours, too."

"You talked to them?"

"I went to see them the night after the game. I told them everything—your relationship to Brian, and to me. I also told them I was pretty crazy about you. And then I realized I'd never told you that."

The hammering in her chest rivaled what the carpenters had been doing earlier.

He walked behind her, reached around the chair's high back and put his hands on her shoulders. "You're important to me, Megan. Despite what you think, I can handle having you in my life. I blew it the other night, but that's not the first time I've done something utterly stupid and thoughtless, and it probably won't be the last. I know I hurt you, but do you really have to give up on me? I promise, I'll try to be more sensitive to your feelings."

The man had a way with words. Now it was she who felt stupid and thoughtless for dwelling on her own injured pride instead of trying to understand what he was going through. "Maybe I was a little hasty," she said, laying her hand atop his where it rested on her shoulder.

With his free hand he tipped her chin up until she was craning her neck, looking up at the ceiling—or rather, up at his face looming upside down over hers. "Does that mean you'll give us another chance?"

She didn't have much choice, not with his lips just inches from hers. He didn't wait for her answer. He closed the gap between them and pressed his lips to hers in a kiss that was both tentative and bone-meltingly intimate.

"Yes, I think we need to try again," she said when he relented. How could she say no when he seemed so earnest? "But you're not exactly playing fair."

"The stakes are too high to play fair," he said as he came around the chair, still holding her hand. He pulled her to her feet and wrapped his arms around her, treating her to a second kiss that was less polite, more demanding.

The front door slammed as the last of the workers left. "Brian's at soccer practice," Holt murmured as he nibbled on Megan's ear. "We have the whole house to ourselves."

"I have an appointment in an hour."

"Cancel it," he said as his hand rode up her thigh beneath her sweater dress.

"I can't. I've been trying to pin this guy down for weeks."

"We'll just have to make do with an hour, then."

"Holt!" But her protest was only halfhearted. Her body had awakened to his touch, and seemingly with a will of its own it sought completion. Her breasts ached and her thighs tingled as liquid heat coursed through her veins. He had been absent from her life for only a few days, yet she was starved for the fulfillment only he could give her.

He started to lift the hem of her dress over her head, but she stopped him. "Don't you think we ought to find a bedroom?"

"Nope. Takes too much time."

"What if Brian comes home early?"

"He won't." The dress was whisked off, and Megan was left standing in her slip, stockings and high heels. Holt untied the orange ribbon, then finger-combed the heavy mass of her hair, arranging it around her bare shoulders, smoothing it across her satin-covered breasts. Then he stood back to admire her.

His gaze roving over her body made her skin flush with heat, but a niggling doubt about Brian prickled at the back of her mind. "How can you be so sure Brian won't—"

"All right, we'll go to the bedroom." Holt smiled indulgently as he picked up her dress and draped it across his shoulder, then took her hand and tugged her toward the stairs. "But let's not waste any time. The minutes are ticking by."

Megan was all too aware of the passing of time. Who could tell when they would next have even a few minutes of privacy? Feeling deliciously naughty, she scampered past Holt and up the stairs. "Race you to the bed." At the top landing she kicked off her heels and darted around the corner to Holt's bedroom.

He caught up with her just as she reached the bed, and they fell onto the mattress in a tangled heap, laughing breathlessly. But the laughter stopped as they kissed again

with an urgency that had nothing to do with time re-
straints.

Megan flicked open his shirt buttons and pressed her
palms against his firm chest, glorying in the latent power
almost humming beneath her hands. He was strong, yet so
gentle as he turned her this way and that in the process of
undressing her. When she was completely bare, he went to
work on his own clothes, stripping off his shirt even as his
gaze remained riveted on her reclining form.

The strength of his desire made her shiver with anticipation. The power of her own response awed her. Her body
needed no coaxing, no slow caresses or warm, wet kisses.
She was ready for him, and the fire in his smoky blue eyes
told her he understood.

She scooted off the bed just long enough for him to throw
the covers back; then they both snuggled into the warm co-
coon provided by a down comforter.

Holt pulled her to him, pressing his face into her hair,
letting her feel his hardness against her thigh.

And then the phone rang.

"Ah, hell," he muttered, glancing over his shoulder toward the interruption with a fierce scowl. "I'm not answering that."

"Maybe you should," Megan said, that odd prickling
thought about Brian prodding her again. "It might be important. What if it's Brian?"

"He'll call back."

Holt tried to resume kissing her as the phone rang six,
seven times, but she had completely lost the mood. Her re-
sponses were halfhearted, and Holt immediately sensed it.

Eight, nine...

"All right, I'll get it." He pulled away and reached behind him to the phone on the nightstand. "Hello?" he
growled. "Yes...yes..."

As he sat up, the irritation on his face melted, forming into a frown of deep concern. Only one thing could prompt that facial expression.

"Is it Brian?" she whispered, pushing herself up onto her knees so she could put her ear close to the phone.

He waved her away. "I'll come immediately" was the last thing he said before hanging up the phone. "That was the soccer coach," he said as he haphazardly threw on his shirt and pants. "Brian was hurt in some sort of accident."

Megan wasted no time locating her own clothes. Her throat constricted when she tried to speak, but she finally managed, "H-how bad is it?"

"I don't know. They took him by ambulance to Woodland. I have to go there now. I'm sorry to leave you like this."

Leave her? *Leave her?* For a moment she was so stunned, she couldn't speak. When she finally did find her voice, she was speaking to thin air; Holt was already halfway down the stairs.

She saw his keys lying on the carpet, where they had probably fallen out of his pants pocket. She grabbed them, pausing on the landing to step into her shoes, then raced down the stairs after Holt.

She found him in the living room, cursing as he searched for his keys.

"I've got them," she said, holding out the silver ring. "And I'm going with you."

He appeared relieved just until the keys were in his hand. "You don't have to come with me," he said. "You've got that important appointment, and—"

"To hell with my appointment! What kind of mother do you think I am, that I would go to a stupid business meeting when my son is in the emergency room?"

He stared at her, blinked a couple of times, then closed his eyes and shook his head. "You're right, of course. Let's go."

Megan's body ran on automatic pilot as she slid into Holt's Porsche and fastened the seat belt. Her mind, meanwhile, was seething. Her fear for Brian's welfare warred with her outrage—no, *outrage* was too mild a word, her *devastation*—over Holt's attitude. Just minutes earlier he had pledged to her that he would be more sensitive to her feelings. Then he'd turned around and done the most *in*sensitive thing she could imagine. She had thought Holt was beginning to see her as having a legitimate role in his family.

Apparently she'd been wrong.

By the time they reached North Dallas, rush hour was hitting its peak and the traffic was stop and go. Holt turned to look at Megan, saw the ravaged look on her face and the barely suppressed tears, and knew he'd made a grave mistake—again.

Damn his thoughtless hide! If he hadn't been in a state of shock after learning of Brian's accident, he wouldn't have rashly dismissed Megan like some insignificant piece of fluff with whom he was having a fling. But sometimes he lost sight of the fact that Megan was Brian's mother. When he was with her, he thought of her as his lover, period. He had neatly compartmentalized her roles within his life, and he was only now realizing how unfair and...unnatural that was.

He reached over and laid his hand over hers. "I'm sorry, Megan. I should have realized how concerned you would be. After all, you are his birth mother—"

"Do you always have to use that adjective when you describe me?" she exploded, pulling away from his touch. "Do I always have to be Brian's *birth* mother? I carried him for nine months, and I struggled through labor with him. A bond formed, and it's never been broken, even during all those years I didn't know he existed. I'm the one who made you answer the phone, because I felt it in my gut that something was wrong. You can deny it all you want, but I am Brian's mother.''

Something inside Holt still rebelled at that statement. On an intellectual level, he knew she was right. But deep down he balked at the concept of Megan as Brian's real mother. As long as he thought of her as a sort of substitute, there was no way she could actually take Shelley's place.

Was that what he feared? In his own mind, Shelley had formed an imprint on his heart that could never be erased. But she was a part of his past, and Megan, he hoped, was his future. He had come to terms with that. But Brian was a different story. As fast as he was growing up, he was still young and impressionable. As he allowed Megan a more and more significant role in his life, was he pushing Shelley's memory aside? If Holt let Megan into his family circle—not as an interloper, but as a true part of the family— wouldn't that be dishonoring Shelley somehow?

Even as these doubts chased each other around in his mind, along with the ever-present fear for Brian's life, Holt knew that he had done Megan an unforgivable disservice. This time it wasn't just a thoughtless gesture he had to make up for, either. It was his whole attitude toward her. She was a mother whose child had been stolen. There was no way she could reclaim those lost years, but now that she had found Brian, she deserved to experience the full spectrum of joys— and sorrows—that went with motherhood.

He swallowed hard. To think he might have lost her because it had taken him too long to understand.... He glanced over at her. Upon seeing that hard, implacable expression on her face, he knew it would take a lot more than a glib apology and a seduction to win her back.

For the next few hours, all of his energy would have to be devoted to Brian. But when the crisis was over, he vowed he would make things right with Megan. He didn't know how yet, but somehow he would do it.

Megan paced the waiting room, emotionally exhausted but too nervous to sit. Each time she walked from one side of the room to the other, she had to step around a baby boy, maybe one year old, who was sprawled on the carpet, engrossed in studying a jack-in-the-box. His mother sat nearby, trying not to nod off.

Megan wondered why they were here, how long they had waited, who in their family was sick or injured.

Both she and Holt had assumed Brian was the victim of an automobile accident, but the injury actually had occurred on the soccer field. A midair collision had resulted in stitches and a concussion for one boy, and for Brian, a compression fracture of the skull and possible spinal damage. He'd been taken into surgery more than an hour ago to relieve the pressure on his brain.

The doctors didn't seem to have any answers. They wouldn't know the extent of brain or spinal damage until Brian regained consciousness.

She never should have urged Holt to allow Brian to play in that league! Holt had tried to explain to her that the play was too intense, the competition too fierce, but she'd been so set on reliving her own athletic triumphs through Brian that she hadn't listened.

Megan spared Holt a glance from time to time. He was slumped in one of those molded plastic chairs, elbows resting on knees, hands clasped, head hanging low. His despair was almost palpable.

They had hardly spoken to each other. At a time when they should have drawn closer for comfort, they were pulling farther apart. Yet she still felt connected to him. Their shared concern for Brian bound them by an invisible cord.

It was silly to let a few hurt feelings stand in the way at a time like this, when they might share their fears and draw strength from each other. Her concerns about her role with the Ramsey family seemed petty when a life hung in the balance.

She sat down next to Holt and laid a hand on his arm in silent commiseration.

He jumped, apparently startled to find her so close to him.

"How are you doing?" she asked. It was a dumb question, but maybe it would open the door for communication.

"Lousy. You?"

"I feel like throwing up. I should have listened when you told me that soccer team was too much for Brian to handle."

Holt looked at her then, his gaze penetrating and full of concern. "Megan, for heaven's sake, it's not your fault. It was just a freak accident. It could have happened anywhere, anytime. And you're not the one who convinced me to let Brian join the Sparks. When the Brewers decided to let Peter join, I was pretty well sunk."

"Oh." She'd actually thought her opinion had swayed him.

"Not that I didn't consider your argument," he added, as if reading her mind. "Anyway, there's no use laying blame. What's done is done. Now we need to apply our energy to—" He looked down suddenly.

Megan's gaze followed his. There was the baby she'd been stepping around earlier, pulling on Holt's shoelaces and sticking the end of one into his mouth.

Holt picked the child up and propped him on his knee. "Hey, there, buddy, where'd you come from?"

The child stared at Holt with a concentrated frown.

"I remember when Brian was this little. Seems like just yesterday."

"What was he like?" Megan asked, stunned to realize she and Holt had never really talked about Brian's early childhood. The subject had seemed so sensitive before; memories of Brian as a little boy would surely include memories of Shelley, as well.

"He was a little monkey, getting into everything," Holt recalled with no hesitation. "He was walking by the time he was nine months old, and he could climb anything. This isn't his first trip to the emergency room, not by a long shot."

"He told me once that he broke his arm in kindergarten."

"And his collarbone in third grade, and his foot in sixth grade. And let's not forget assorted gashes requiring various numbers of stitches, and a run-in with a nest of yellow jackets."

"So you're an old hand at this emergency room stuff."

He shook his head. "No way. You never get used to it."

"Tell me more about him when he was little," she said, because talking seemed to help. "What were his favorite toys? Did he have a security blanket? An imaginary friend?"

Holt actually managed a smile. "His imaginary friend was Conan the Barbarian. And he didn't have a blanket, but he had a security pillow. I thought we'd never get it away from him." He paused, hesitating over his next words. "You know, I have a bunch of photo albums. I'm surprised you never asked to see them."

"I intended to. But I knew that pictures of Brian would naturally include pictures of Shelley, and I wasn't sure if you were ready for that. No, that's not the whole truth," she added hastily. "I wasn't sure *I* was ready."

He stared at her. "What do you mean?"

She took the nameless baby from Holt, giving her something to focus on as she formulated an answer. "I guess I was afraid of an unflattering comparison. I know she must have been a wonderful wife and mother, but I wasn't ready to see the hard evidence of just how wonderful. Family photos provide such an intimate look into people's lives...."

"Shelley was wonderful, I can't deny that. But so are you."

As a substitute, she wanted to add. But maybe that was just her insecurities talking. "I'd like to see the photos," she said. "But I'd rather hear you talk about Brian. What was his first day of school like?"

And so they talked, passing the baby back and forth. The young mother would be horrified when she woke up, Megan thought, once she realized she'd fallen asleep and left her baby at the mercy of total strangers. But the poor woman looked so exhausted, Megan didn't have the heart to wake her.

The time seemed to pass a little more quickly. Megan went to get them coffee, and when she returned, the baby was once again in his drowsy mother's care, and Holt was speaking to a doctor in green scrubs.

"Brian's out of surgery," Holt reported to Megan as she walked up. "He came through fine. This is Dr. Lewis, the surgeon. Doctor, this is Megan Carlisle."

Megan handed one cup of coffee to Holt so she could shake hands with the doctor.

"They're taking him to the Neurosurgical Intensive Care Unit," Dr. Lewis said.

"Can he have visitors?" Megan asked.

He hesitated. "Yes, but only immediate family."

"Megan *is* immediate family," Holt interjected, taking her hand in a painfully tight grasp. "She's Brian's mother."

Eleven

———

Megan threw Holt a look of gratitude for allowing her to come with him to see Brian. She knew it must have been hard for him to outwardly acknowledge her in the role of Brian's mother. He loosened the death grip he had on her hand and gave her an encouraging smile.

Dr. Lewis escorted them all the way to the Neurosurgical ICU, explaining the extent of Brian's known injuries. Some of the complicated medical jargon flew right over Megan's head, but she didn't ask for clarification. It all sounded horrible and painful; she didn't want to hear any more nightmarish details than absolutely necessary.

But no matter how thorough the doctor's explanation, it didn't prepare her for the sight that met her when she reached Brian's bedside. Emotion clutched at her throat as she viewed her child, small and frail-looking in the big hospital bed, hooked up to every conceivable sort of machine, including a ventilator. His head was wrapped up in bandages, and he had a big collar around his neck that looked worse than anything Dr. Frankenstein could have dreamed up.

"Oh, God," Holt said. The two quietly uttered words reflected so much despair that Megan wanted to cry for him as well as Brian. But she didn't cry. Both Ramsey men would need her to be strong.

"He came through the surgery like a trooper," Dr. Lewis said. "Don't let all these wires scare you. They're connected to monitors so we can track his vital signs, which right now are looking very strong. The ventilator is used to increase the oxygen in his blood, which helps to keep pressure off his brain."

"When will he wake up?" Megan asked, her voice faltering.

"It's hard to say. As we withdraw the sedative he's on, he should wake up on his own, but sometimes it takes a while."

Holt posed the question Megan was too scared to ask. "Brian *will* wake up, won't he?"

Dr. Lewis didn't answer right away. "I expect him to. But there's always a slight chance he'll slip deeper. Head injuries are unpredictable."

Coma. The unspoken word reverberated through the room as though someone had shouted it. Holt reached blindly for Megan's hand, again squeezing so hard, she thought the bones in her fingers would snap. Oddly comforted by his intensity, she didn't object.

After their initial visit, Megan and Holt were allowed to visit Brian only ten minutes every two hours. The rest of the time they waited in a small visitor lounge, saying little to each other, passing the time by drinking gallons of coffee and thinking, just thinking.

Only hours before Brian had been running and laughing. Now he was so still.

Megan rediscovered prayers she hadn't offered since childhood, and she made up a few more for good measure. During the brief times they were allowed to sit by the bed, she talked aloud to Brian, offering words of encouragement that she hoped would somehow penetrate his unconscious state.

He had to wake up and be okay. He had his whole life to live. Surely God wouldn't claim Holt's son so soon after taking his wife. Surely He wouldn't give her a miracle—the return of her child—only to snatch it away.

Holt checked his watch. It was three minutes to eight in the morning. Then he surreptitiously checked Megan. The shadows beneath her eyes spoke of her exhaustion. He almost suggested that she go home for a short rest, but he knew she wouldn't leave the hospital unless she was forced to.

He felt the same way. Their shared vigil had formed a bond between them—a parenting bond Holt had never thought he would share with anyone but Shelley. Rather than feeling threatened by Megan's growing devotion to his family, he welcomed the connection. If anything could bring about Brian's recovery, the strength of both his and Megan's love for their son could.

Their son. They might not have conceived him together, but Brian was their son from this night on.

He scooted his chair closer to Megan's. "Why don't you lay your head on my shoulder and doze for a while?" he suggested. "I'll wake you if there's any news."

She looked at him, then bit her lower lip and looked away uncertainly. He knew how she felt—like the second they let down their guard, something bad might happen.

"It'll be okay," he said.

She sighed. "I suppose I ought to try to get some sleep. I'm getting kind of punchy. A few minutes ago, when we were in with Brian, I thought I saw a face peering through the glass from outside the ward... you know, out of the corner of my eye. Then when I looked, it was gone." She laid her head tentatively against his shoulder. "Maybe we can take turns napping."

"Okay. You go first." He slid his arm around her, reassured by the warmth of her nearness in the chilly waiting room. Within a couple of minutes he felt her muscles relaxing and her breathing becoming deep and even.

Unfortunately she didn't sleep long. In less than half an hour she awoke with a start, then yawned and rubbed her eyes. "This is no good. I'll end up in traction if I sleep for long with my neck crooked like that. I think I'll go splash some water on my face."

"It's almost time for us to visit Brian again."

"I know. I'll be back in just a minute."

Holt watched her go, wishing he could do more for her. But he wasn't in any better shape than she was. His eyes burned from lack of sleep.

When visiting time rolled around and Megan still hadn't returned, Holt didn't wait. She would be along in a minute, he was sure. He smiled at Brian's nurse as he approached the bed. "Any changes?"

She shook her head.

Holt settled into a chair. Where was Megan? He realized he didn't like sitting here without her. He felt more afraid.

He closed his eyes, just for a moment. In the quiet of early morning, the memories came more easily. He could clearly picture some of the scenes he had described to Megan while they waited through the surgery—Brian taking his first steps, learning how to swim, riding his first two-wheeler.

Most vivid was the memory of Brian falling out of the big tree in the backyard, only five years old and trying to pretend he wasn't hurt. He hadn't cried much until he'd seen the inside of the hospital. But in the face of all those bright lights, X-ray machines and strange people in white, his brave facade had crumbled.

Don't let 'em hurt me, Dad, he'd sobbed. *Please, Dad, take me home. Dad! Dad!* "Dad?"

Holt's eyes jerked open. He'd been dreaming, but the voice had sounded so real—

"Dad?"

He nearly knocked the chair over as he leapt out of it and peered into Brian's face. His eyes were open.

"What happened?" Brian asked in a thready voice, blinking in confusion.

"Oh, thank God." Holt nearly fell to the floor with relief. "You're in the hospital. You were at practice, and you had a head-on collision with a guy named Bubba. Do you remember?"

"Sort of. My head...hurts."

Holt tried not to wince at the understatement. "I'm not surprised." He wasn't sure if he should tell Brian yet about the surgery. The idea of a hole in his skull might upset him.

"Is Meg here?" Brian asked anxiously. He couldn't move his head, but his eyes darted back and forth. "I thought...I guess I must have been dreaming or something."

Holt smiled. "She's been here the whole time, talking to you. She went to wash her face. She'll be right back."

Brian seemed to relax slightly. "How long have I been here?"

"About eighteen hours."

"That's unreal."

When Brian had first spoken, his nurse had immediately called for the doctor on duty. Holt was ushered out into the hallway to wait as the medical personnel pulled the curtain around Brian's bed and conducted their examination. Holt looked toward the coffee machine, wondering what was keeping Megan, but the hallway was deserted.

He heard footsteps behind him and turned to find her approaching from the opposite direction, carrying two steaming paper cups. "I figured as long as I was up and around, I'd get us some cof—" She halted, took one look through the glass at the curtains drawn around Brian's bed and the flurry of activity going on and dropped both cups. They splatted loudly as they hit the floor, coffee flying everywhere.

"Oh my God, what happened?"

He should have realized she might misunderstand. "No, no, Megan, honey, it's good," he quickly reassured her. "Brian woke up."

"You mean he's okay? Could he talk? Was he in pain?"

"He said he had a headache. And he asked for you, first thing. A doctor is checking him out. He's groggy, but other than that he seemed—" Holt couldn't resist smiling "—pretty normal."

Megan hadn't cried once during the whole ordeal, at least not in front of him, but now she burst into unabashed tears. Holt took her in his arms and held her close, rubbing her back, knowing he would never forget this moment of sharing joy and relief. He felt closer to Megan than he ever had before, even closer than when they had made love and it had seemed their souls had brushed. He couldn't help but marvel at how whole and complete he suddenly felt.

And he couldn't help but realize that this was a fleeting moment, and that if he didn't do something, she would slip away from him. Right now their shared concern for Brian was all that kept them together.

The doctor emerged as Holt and Megan were cleaning up the spilled coffee, and his report was encouraging. His preliminary examination revealed no abnormalities, no paralysis or obvious impairments. More elaborate tests would have to be performed, he cautioned them, but he was smiling.

Megan and Holt were allowed a short visit until the nurse chased them out, insisting that Brian needed rest and absolute calm.

Throughout the rest of the morning, Brian, although groggy, responded to their visits. He was taken off the respirator. He underwent a CAT scan, the results of which were promising. By noon, Dr. Lewis declared that Brian was out of immediate danger, and that if he continued his meteoric improvement, he could be taken out of intensive care that evening. Brian himself insisted that Holt and Megan go home and get some sleep.

"He's right," Holt said to Megan. "We won't be any good to Brian if we're both jabbering idiots."

Megan reluctantly agreed. After leaving the nurse their phone numbers, they headed for Holt's car.

The autumn air was crisp. Holt took several deep, cleansing breaths to wash the hospital smell out of his nose.

"Your apartment is closer," he said as he and Megan made their way across the visitor parking lot. "I'll drop you off. You can pick up your car at my house later."

"Why don't we both go to my place?" she suggested. "You won't be able to sleep at your house with the carpenters and their hammers and their radio."

He shuddered. "What a gruesome thought. Sure you don't mind?" He shot her a mischievous smile, testing the waters, hoping against hope that, in light of all they'd shared this night, Megan could forget the stupid things he'd done in the past.

But it wasn't going to be that simple.

"If I thought there was even a remote chance either one of us could do more than sleep, I might give it a second thought. But at this point, I'm only trying to be practical."

He decided he wouldn't tell her there was more than a remote chance. He might be exhausted, but with Brian out of the woods he felt like celebrating. One tiny nod from Megan and he'd be only too happy to take up where they'd left off before that harrowing phone call.

But Megan was asleep almost before her head hit the pillow. Holt stretched out beside her in her Art Deco bed, fully clothed and fully aroused. It was a long time before sleep claimed him.

Megan awoke in the warm security of Holt's embrace. Her back was against his chest, his arms were wrapped tightly around her shoulders, and her head was tucked under his chin. She'd never awakened next to him before; circumstances hadn't allowed them to spend an entire night together. She marveled at how wonderful it felt.

Then she realized she still wore her orange sweater dress and panty hose, and her pleasure dissipated. She and Holt were sleeping on the same bed for convenience' sake, she reminded herself. They weren't even under the covers. During the all-night hospital vigil she had pushed aside the blow Holt had dealt her, but now she recalled with painful vividness the casual way he had dismissed her after learning of Brian's accident.

She might as well face it. Holt would never fully accept her as Brian's mother. It wasn't his fault. He cared for her, and he wanted to be fair with her, but she couldn't expect him to let her replace Shelley. Holt, Shelley and Brian had been a family for twelve years—a perfect triangle. Perfect triangles came along once in a lifetime.

She could tell Holt was asleep by his regular breathing, but even in sleep, the strength of his desire was evident. His hardness pressed against her bottom, and she had to fight the impulse to turn in his arms and kiss him slowly awake. But those few minutes of ecstasy they might share would only compromise the decision she'd reached.

Carefully she slid out of Holt's embrace. He shifted, made a sleepy noise of protest, then stilled. She brushed a lock of hair from his forehead. Such a good man. She couldn't stay angry with him. He couldn't help how he felt. She could even admire him for his loyalty to Shelley.

Megan tiptoed out of the room, then went straight to the phone in the kitchen and called the hospital. Brian was asleep, but his nurse reported that he was doing even better than expected.

Cheered by the news, Megan took a quick shower and threw on some clean clothes, moving quietly around in the bedroom as Holt slept on. She checked in at her office and started fixing something to eat. Only then did she wake Holt.

"Mmm, what time is it?" he asked muzzily after she'd lightly jiggled his shoulder.

"Almost five. I figured four hours' sleep was enough to keep us going for a while." She updated him on what she'd learned about Brian.

"Great, that's great." He squeezed his eyes shut, then opened them and stared blearily at her. "You look chipper. Don't tell me you're one of those cheery, bounce-out-of-bed morning people. If so, we'll never suit."

They would never suit for more reasons than her wake-up habits, but she decided to keep the mood light. "Don't tell me you're one of those grouchy, don't-talk-to-me-'til-I've-had-my-coffee people," she countered. "Total incompatibility."

He didn't deny her accusation. "Is that bacon I smell?"

"And toast, eggs, coffee and orange juice. I don't know about you, but I'm starving. We haven't eaten anything substantial since lunch yesterday."

He sat up and swung his bare feet to the floor, grinning. "You're forgiven for being cheerful."

As they quickly demolished the food, Megan made small talk. She could hear the strain in her own voice, but Holt either didn't notice or chose not to comment. If she could just make it through the next few hours, once she was sure Brian was really okay, she could come home—alone—and have her own private nervous breakdown.

"Hi, Meg," Brian said as Megan entered the private room to which he'd been transferred. His voice was still weak, but he seemed more alert than he had earlier.

"How did you know it was me?" she asked as she came closer and leaned over the bed so Brian could see her face. "With that thing around your neck, you can't see anything but the ceiling."

"I don't know. Your perfume, maybe. Where's Dad?"

"He'll be along in a few minutes. He wanted to take a shower and change clothes. How do you feel?"

"Terrible. They give me this pain medicine that makes me feel like I'm swimming through Jell-O. And the dreams! I thought…this probably sounds stupid, but I thought I was talking to my grandmother."

About the same time Brian revealed this interesting tidbit, Megan's gaze focused on a huge green plant wrapped in purple foil, sitting on the windowsill. She walked around the bed to have a closer look.

"She was singing a song," he continued, "something about a meadow and turtles and fish and bees and rats, I swear."

Megan gasped. She knew that song. In a halting voice, she sang the first few lines.

"That's it!" Brian said in amazement. "How'd you know?"

"Because she used to sing the same song to me when I was sick." Megan recalled the fleeting image of a face peeking through the window in ICU the night before. She'd thought it a hallucination, but now she wasn't so sure. "Oh, Brian, I think she really must have been here. There's a pretty plant on the windowsill that doesn't have a card, but I'll bet she brought it."

"Really?"

"I didn't tell you this before, but your grandmother has been keeping tabs on you. She came to one of your soccer games, maybe more than one. She wanted to meet you, but she was afraid."

"Afraid? Why?"

"Because she knew my father wouldn't approve, and she's very loyal to him, even after learning some of the terrible things he did. I think she was also afraid that maybe you wouldn't like her."

"That's dumb."

Megan laughed. "Not so dumb, really. I felt like that, too, at one time."

Brian pursed his lips. "I wish she'd come back."

"I think she will," Megan said, praying she was right. She wasn't even sure how her mother had learned of the accident, unless she'd been there watching from a distance. Megan had tried to call her once, but hadn't been able to get an answer. But Rolanda must have been in this room. How else would Brian have known about that song?

The door opened and Holt walked in, carrying a loaded shopping bag. "Hey, Bri. You're awake."

"Hey, Dad."

"What's in the bag?" Megan asked.

"Video games. Comic books. And…" With a flourish he pulled from the bag the ugliest stuffed frog Megan had ever seen, and held it up so Brian could see. "Mr. Cheeks."

Brian looked mortified. "Aw, Dad!"

Megan stifled a giggle. "Who's Mr. Cheeks?"

"Shelley bought him for Brian when he had the mumps," Holt replied.

"When I was eight," Brian added. "Jeez, where did you dig him up?"

"From under your bed. I seem to recall your having a fit a couple of years ago when I wanted to throw him away."

Brian rolled his eyes. "All right, give him here." Holt set the stuffed frog on Brian's chest, and Brian gave it a dutiful pat. "But I don't think I'm ready for video games. My eyes won't even focus."

"What makes you think I brought those for you? Maybe Megan and I will play them when you're asleep."

"Yeah, right. Hey, Dad, can I talk to you? Alone, I mean."

Megan's heart constricted. Brian had never excluded her like that before. But his attitude only served to underscore her status within the Ramsey family.

She did a masterful job hiding her pain. "Oh, um, I'll just run along," she said. "I'll see if I can't track down your mysterious visitor."

Brian smiled. "Thanks, Meg."

Holt felt a pang of concern as Megan left. "What is it, Brian? What couldn't you say in front of Megan?"

Brian took his time answering. "I almost died, didn't I?"

Holt took a deep breath. "You scared us, that's for sure."

"After the accident…" He hesitated again, then blurted out, "I saw Mom. Or maybe it was just a dream, but it seemed so real. It was just like in the movies. There was a long, dark tunnel with a bright light at the end, and Mom was standing there in the light, and she looked real beautiful, like before she was sick.''

Holt swallowed the lump in his throat. ''Did she say anything?''

''Yeah. She said she was sorry she couldn't be with us. And then she said she would always be my mother, but that...promise you won't get mad?''

''Why would I get mad?''

''You just might.''

''I promise I won't. What did she say?''

''Well, she said Meg was my real mother, too, and that it was okay for me to have two real moms.'' Brian waited for Holt's reaction.

Holt cleared his throat. ''It *is* okay. When I said Megan wasn't your real mother, that was before I knew her. She's a fine person, and she deserves...well, she deserves better than she's gotten, I think.'' Better than he'd given her.

''Yeah. She got a real raw deal. Sometimes she seems so sad. I wish there was something we could do for her.''

''There might be,'' Holt murmured. ''Uh, what else did Mom say?''

''That's all I remember. It was probably just a dream, but I still feel like she was closer than she's been in a long time. That's why I didn't want to tell you in front of Meg. I was afraid she would...I don't know, get her feelings hurt or something, like I was wanting Mom to be here instead of her. But that's not true at all. I...I love them both.''

''You know something?'' Holt said. ''So do I. But I do a lousy job of showing it.'' He thought back to the way he'd acted when he got the phone call about Brian's accident, and cringed.

The door opened again, and a stocky blond teenage boy stuck his head around the corner. ''Brian?''

"Come in, Peter," Holt said.

"Oh, hi, Mr. Ramsey." The boy's eyes grew huge as he regarded his friend and the impressive array of hardware attached to him. "Oh, wow, man, you look awful."

"So do you, but at least I have an excuse. And don't say a word about the frog, or I'll have to kill you."

Sure that Brian was in good company for the next several minutes, Holt left in search of Megan. He'd wasted enough time worrying about all the wrong things. Maybe he couldn't right the injustices of Megan's past, but he could take his best damn shot at securing a happy future for her.

Twelve

Rolanda had to be lurking in that hospital somewhere; Megan just knew it. But she had tried every waiting room she could think of, with no luck. She had all but given up the search when she unexpectedly stumbled across her mother—in the cafeteria, of all places, wolfing down a hamburger like it was her last meal. She looked very un-Rolanda-like wearing plain cotton slacks and a pullover sweater. Her hair was slicked back in a ponytail, and she wore little if any makeup.

Megan got herself yet another cup of coffee, then plopped down in a chair across from her mother.

Rolanda looked up, and for a moment she said nothing, but her eyes swam with tears. "Oh, Megan, he looks so awful. Will he be all right?"

Megan covered her mother's hands with hers. "I just came from his room. He was awake and already sounds better than he did just a few hours ago. How did you find out about the accident? I tried calling you, but—"

"I was there," Rolanda said solemnly. "I was parked at the curb, watching the team practice, when those two kids went for the ball at the same time and butted heads like a couple of bighorn sheep. I went to a pay phone and called your office, but they couldn't get hold of you."

"I was at Holt's. The coach called."

"Anyway, as I watched them load that limp little body into the ambulance, I realized how stupid I was being, hiding in the shadows to watch Brian. I kept thinking, what if he dies? It'll be too late. He's my grandchild, perhaps the only one I'll have, and I've let stupid, blind loyalty keep me away—loyalty to a man who doesn't even remotely deserve it."

Megan was shocked. She'd never heard her mother say anything so negative about her father.

"It's true," Rolanda continued. "The more I think about it, the more I realize what a rotten person Cramer was."

"Mother!"

"Perhaps I shouldn't speak ill of the dead, but it's time I faced the facts. Cramer didn't love us, he dominated us."

"He cared for us in his own way," Megan argued, somewhat insincerely. But she felt compelled to defend her father, if only for her mother's sake. Cramer had been her whole life.

"He cared for us the way a man cares for possessions, not people," Rolanda said bitterly. "But it's over now. He's not around to disapprove of anything I do. I still have a good portion of my life left, God willing, and I'm going to start living it. After getting reacquainted with my daughter, my next order of business is to get to know my grandson. That is, if it's okay with you and Holt."

"Mother, of course it's okay. I know you were with Brian this morning. You sang that song, 'Over in the Meadow.'"

Rolanda nervously twisted her wedding ring. "I didn't think he was awake."

"He only remembers it vaguely. But he wants to meet you. Come on, finish your hamburger and I'll walk upstairs with you. Holt and Brian kicked me out so they could have a little man-to-man talk, but they must be done by now."

Rolanda smiled, pushing the unfinished hamburger away. "You don't sound very happy about that."

"Oh, I'm just being childish. I never have liked anyone to keep secrets from me."

Holt, to his credit, didn't make a big deal of it when Megan entered Brian's room with her mother in tow. "Hello, Mrs. Carlisle, it's nice to see you again."

She acknowledged him cautiously, and then her gaze fixed on the bed. "Hello, Brian."

"H-hi," Brian said uncertainly. "You're my grandmother."

"Yes, that's right. Not that I've really earned that title, but I'm going to try. Do you feel like talking?"

"Sure, I guess. Thanks for the plant. Meg showed it to me."

"You're welcome. That was kind of a dumb present to get, you being the son of a nursery owner and all. I mean, your dad could get you thousands of plants."

"It's okay. I like plants."

Megan nodded toward the door, and she and Holt slipped outside so grandmother and grandson could get better acquainted.

"You look worried," Megan observed. "You don't mind Mother suddenly showing up, do you?"

"No, not at all. Brian's never had a grandmother before."

"My mother's never *been* a grandmother before. It should be interesting. You're still frowning."

"Does this hospital have a chapel?"

"It's on the first floor. Why? Do you want to pray?"

"Actually, most of my prayers have already been answered. All but one." He took her hand. "I just want to go someplace quiet. Will you come with me?"

"All right."

Holt said nothing more until they'd found the peaceful little chapel. It smelled of flowers and beeswax. They slipped into a back pew and knelt for a few minutes. He offered a prayer of thanks for Brian's life, and he suspected Megan did the same.

An elderly man, the chapel's only other occupant, rose from his seat in front and left, nodding silently to them on his way out.

"I guess I've really messed things up," Holt said as they settled into the pew. Although they were now alone, he whispered.

"It's okay," Megan whispered back. "I'm not angry anymore. I understand how things are."

"No, I don't think you do." He took her hand again. "Life has thrown you and me some rotten curves. Families have been torn apart, people taken from us. But there's no reason we can't start fresh...." No, no, no, those weren't the words he wanted to say at all. But how could he possibly convey what he felt for Megan? "Aren't you even going to ask what my one unanswered prayer is?" he finally asked. Waiting for her reply, his heart hammered so loudly, he was sure she could hear it.

"All right. What is it?"

"Megan Carlisle, you would make me very happy if you would marry me."

She stared at him, her face revealing nothing. Oh, God, what was going through her mind? Had his earlier thoughtlessness torn them apart irrevocably?

"I know Brian would approve," he said to fill the silence. "He loves you very much."

"I...I love him, too," she said, her voice barely audible. "But...I can't marry you." She looked as if she'd stunned even herself with her answer. "I know Brian needs a stable mother figure, and I'd like to oblige, but I have to think of my needs, too. And I could never be happy as a...a substitute, a second-class family member."

Holt was horrified. He was the one who'd made her feel that way. "No, Megan, you've got it all wrong! I'll admit that, for a time, I was worried that you would somehow replace Shelley—not in my heart, but in Brian's. That's why I stayed away whenever the two of you were together. I figured as long as we didn't act like a family, Shelley's status would be protected. It sounds crazy now, but that's what was going on in my head."

"It's not crazy," she said. "I understood, probably before you did. What you had with Shelley was special. I can't expect—"

"Megan, will you listen? Everything has changed. And it took a fourteen-year-old boy, in all his infinite wisdom, to make me see what a jackass I've been."

"You haven't been a jackass," she insisted. "You were only following your heart."

He gave her shoulders a gentle shake. "That's exactly what the problem was—my heart. For a while, I felt like it was tearing in two. Part of it wanted to remain with Shelley, the other wanted to make room for you. Then Brian reminded me that hearts don't come in a finite size. There's plenty of room in his for two moms, both of them very real. And there's plenty of room in mine, too. Shelley was dear to me, and I'll always honor her memory, both for the feelings we shared and for all she gave to Brian."

A glimmer of understanding shone in Megan's eyes, giving him hope. "I wish I'd known her."

"I wish you had, too," he said wistfully. "You two would have been great friends. But, Megan, honey, you're the one I love now. I love you more than I can even put into words."

"I love you, too," she said, her voice thick with tears.

"I was scared at first by how hard and fast I fell for you, but now I know that my feelings for you can't tarnish Shelley's memory in any way, not for me or Brian. We can form a new family, the three of us. It won't be the same family as when Shelley was with us, but that doesn't mean it'll be a poor substitute, either. It'll just be different—wonderful and different."

"How can you know that?" she asked. "We've just been through a very emotional experience. You might not feel the same way tomorrow."

"Yes, I will. Megan, please think about it. After the things I've done, I don't blame you for doubting me. But I'll earn back your trust, I swear it. Just don't say no."

In all her years, Megan had never heard a more earnest declaration. "All right, I'll think about it," she said. She felt rotten, giving him such a stingy crumb after all the beautiful things he'd said, but her self-preservation instincts wouldn't allow her to snatch up the hope he'd offered her. What if he was wrong?

He smiled anyway. "Thanks." He cupped her face in his hands and kissed her so sweetly, she wanted to melt into a puddle. She imagined kissing him not in a hospital chapel, but in the big white church where her family belonged, with all of their friends and relatives in attendance. The image became so vivid, it made her dizzy, and she clutched his arms for support.

"Maybe we should go back upstairs and see how Brian and Mother are getting along," she said.

Holt nodded.

They were in the elevator halfway to the fifth floor when it hit her. She was being a fool. Maybe the situation wasn't picture perfect, but what marriage was? They had a damn good start—their love for Brian, and for each other. Holt had lost his first wife, but he was willing to risk loving again. She knew he would try his very hardest to make her happy. Couldn't she put aside her fears and try, too?

She turned to look at him. His face was hard, resolute, and she knew he was not so much disappointed in her answer as angry with himself for causing her doubts. Lord, hadn't they both suffered enough? Had she been so miserable for so many years that she couldn't recognize potential happiness when it slapped her in the face?

"Holt."

He looked at her, his eyes filled with questions.

"I've thought about your proposal. And my answer is yes."

He stared at her long and hard, as if he couldn't believe his ears. Then abruptly he pulled her into a bone-crushing hug. "Megan, honey, are you sure?" he murmured into her hair. "If you need more time..."

"I don't have to think anymore. If I had any doubts, they were more due to my insecurities than anything. I've always been a little jealous of Shelley, for the things she enjoyed that I missed. But you and I, we're the future. I've got to stop mourning the things I lost, and rejoice in what I've been given. I'm so lucky. You and Brian are the best family a woman could ask for."

"No, *I'm* the lucky one," he said, squeezing her tightly.

The elevator doors opened and closed again, but Holt and Megan didn't move. Megan never wanted to move; she never wanted to lose the closeness she felt with Holt at that moment. She could feel his love engulfing her and the answering pulse of her own deepest feelings.

The elevator opened again. Reluctantly they pulled apart and exited, but the closeness remained. Holt was inside of Megan, a part of her soul. Whether they were standing next to each other or miles apart, they would remain heart to heart. She smiled up at him, glowing inside.

Figuring Brian had had enough excitement for one day, what with the sudden appearance of his grandmother, Holt and Megan waited until the next day to tell him of their engagement.

"All right!" Brian said, raising his fist in the air in a gesture of triumph and very nearly dislodging his IV. "I knew it. I knew it all along. But you have to wait until my hair grows back out. I'm not going to the wedding looking like a dufus."

"I imagine we can wait that long," Holt said. "We were thinking maybe around Christmas."

"Christmas!" Rolanda exploded. "You expect me to put together a wedding in less than three months?"

"Mother, it's not going to be an elaborate ceremony," Megan objected. "Small and tasteful, family and close friends only."

"But you'll have to reserve the church! And the country club for the reception. Do you have any idea how booked up they get around Christmas?"

"If the church can't accommodate us, we can do the whole thing at the house," Megan argued calmly. "But we aren't waiting any longer than we have to."

Rolanda looked to Holt for confirmation. When no one else joined her in the argument, she slumped back into her chair and smiled despite herself. "You're right. I don't know what I was thinking. Lord knows you've waited long enough, Megan."

Megan relaxed, too. She'd been worried that her mother would try to turn her wedding into the social event of the season, but apparently she hadn't sunk her teeth too deeply into that idea.

"Why don't you two run along and get some rest?" Rolanda suggested. "You've been camped out at this hospital for two days. I'll stay with Brian. He promised to show me how to play his video games."

Megan bit her lip to keep from laughing. Rolanda and video games? What was the world coming to?

"I think we will go home for a while," Holt said. Then he looked at Megan and winked. "There's something I have to show you."

During the drive to his home in Lakewood, Megan tried to pry the surprise out of him, but he wouldn't give her even a hint. Maybe it was an engagement ring. No, when would he have had time to buy one? Anyway, knowing Holt, he would want her to pick out the ring.

After pulling the car into the garage, he made Megan close her eyes. He led her inside, twirled her around a bit to confuse her, then finally released her.

"Okay, you can open your eyes."

She did, finding herself standing in the middle of the kitchen—the beautiful, completely finished kitchen.

"My word, when did this happen?" she asked, her mouth hanging open as she turned slowly around to view the final results. The cabinet doors were hung, the shiny new appliances were installed and Holt's heirloom table—the focal point of the whole kitchen—had been refinished and returned to its rightful place. Everything was immaculate, as if the workers had never been there.

"Your friend Sheena took over. She had those carpenters jumping around here like fleas."

"I told you Sheena was good. If you'd let her do the whole job in the first place, she probably would have had it completed on schedule. Do you . . . like it?"

"I love it. I can already see you here, fixing dinner every night—"

"Whoa, whoa, negative. *We'll* be fixing dinner. All of us. You and Brian are going to learn to cook."

He had the good grace to look ashamed. "Yes, ma'am. As long as you're the instructor."

She nodded, satisfied that she wasn't about to marry a male chauvinist pig.

"Well, now," Holt said, "since you've done such a magnificent job on the kitchen, what room do you want to start on next?"

She pretended to give the matter deep consideration. Then she walked slowly up to Holt and wound her arms around his neck, her mind full of mischief. "The bedroom. Definitely the bedroom. But I'd like to check it out, first, you know, see how things work, so I can better evaluate your needs."

"Our needs." He smiled wickedly as he ran one hand down the length of her body and cupped her bottom suggestively. "After the bedroom, then what?"

"How about a nursery?"

He grinned like an idiot, and she knew that was the answer he'd been looking for.

*   *   *   *   *

MILLION DOLLAR SWEEPSTAKES (III)

No purchase necessary. To enter, follow the directions published. Method of entry may vary. For eligibility, entries must be received no later than March 31, 1996. No liability is assumed for printing errors, lost, late or misdirected entries. Odds of winning are determined by the number of eligible entries distributed and received. Prizewinners will be determined no later than June 30, 1996.

Sweepstakes open to residents of the U.S. (except Puerto Rico), Canada, Europe and Taiwan who are 18 years of age or older. All applicable laws and regulations apply. Sweepstakes offer void wherever prohibited by law. Values of all prizes are in U.S. currency. This sweepstakes is presented by Torstar Corp., its subsidiaries and affiliates, in conjunction with book, merchandise and/or product offerings. For a copy of the Official Rules send a self-addressed, stamped envelope (WA residents need not affix return postage) to: MILLION DOLLAR SWEEPSTAKES (III) Rules, P.O. Box 4573, Blair, NE 68009, USA.

EXTRA BONUS PRIZE DRAWING

No purchase necessary. The Extra Bonus Prize will be awarded in a random drawing to be conducted no later than 5/30/96 from among all entries received. To qualify, entries must be received by 3/31/96 and comply with published directions. Drawing open to residents of the U.S. (except Puerto Rico), Canada, Europe and Taiwan who are 18 years of age or older. All applicable laws and regulations apply; offer void wherever prohibited by law. Odds of winning are dependent upon number of eligible entries received. Prize is valued in U.S. currency. The offer is presented by Torstar Corp., its subsidiaries and affiliates in conjunction with book, merchandise and/or product offering. For a copy of the Official Rules governing this sweepstakes, send a self-addressed, stamped envelope (WA residents need not affix return postage) to: Extra Bonus Prize Drawing Rules, P.O. Box 4590, Blair, NE 68009, USA.

SWP-S994

SILHOUETTE®

Desire®

Big Bad
WOLFE

WOLFE WANTING
by Joan Hohl

Don't miss *Wolfe Wanting*, Book 3 of Joan Hohl's
seductively sexy BIG BAD WOLFE series, coming your
way in October...only from Silhouette Desire.

As sergeant for the Pennsylvania State Police
Department, Royce Wolfe was just doing his job—
protecting a violent-crime victim, making sure she
was safe. But he deserved a slap in the face for what
he was thinking about the sexy woman. He wanted
her—bad. But a Big *Bad* Wolfe was the last thing
Megan Delaney needed....

SDJH3

Premiere

The stars are out in October at Silhouette! Read captivating love stories by talented *new* authors— in their very first Silhouette appearance.

Sizzle with Susan Crosby's
THE MATING GAME—Desire #888
...when Iain Mackenzie and Kani Warner are forced to spend their days—and *nights*—together in *very* close tropical quarters!

Explore the passion in Sandra Moore's
HIGH COUNTRY COWBOY—Special Edition #918
...where Jake Valiteros tries to control the demons that haunt him—along with a stubborn woman as wild as the Wyoming wind.

Cherish the emotion in Kia Cochrane's
MARRIED BY A THREAD—Intimate Moments #600
...as Dusty McKay tries to recapture the love he once shared with his wife, Tori.

Exhilarate in the power of Christie Clark's
TWO HEARTS TOO LATE—Romance #1041
...as Kirby Anne Gordon and Carl Tannon fight for custody of a small child...and battle their growing attraction!

Shiver with Val Daniels'
BETWEEN DUSK AND DAWN—Shadows #42
...when a mysterious stranger claims to want to save Jonna Sanders from a serial killer.

Catch the classics of tomorrow—*premiering* today—
Only from

Silhouette®

SILHOUETTE® *Desire®*

ANNETTE BROADRICK'S
SONS OF TEXAS
SERIES CONTINUES

Available in October from Silhouette Desire, TEMPTATION TEXAS STYLE! (SD #883) is the latest addition to Annette Broadrick's series about the Callaway family.

Roughed-up rodeo cowboy Tony Callaway thought women were nothing but trouble—but once this lonesome cowboy took one look into Christina O'Reilly's sultry green eyes, he was sure to change his mind!

Don't miss Tony Callaway's story in TEMPTATION TEXAS STYLE! by Annette Broadrick, Desire's MAN OF THE MONTH for October.

He's one of the SONS OF TEXAS and
ready to ride into your heart!

Jilted!

Left at the altar, but not for long.

Why are these six couples
who have sworn off love
suddenly hearing wedding bells?

Find out in these scintillating books
by your favorite authors,
coming this November!

#889 THE ACCIDENTAL BRIDEGROOM
by Ann Major
(Man of the Month)

#890 TWO HEARTS, SLIGHTLY USED
by Dixie Browning

#891 THE BRIDE SAYS NO
by Cait London

#892 SORRY, THE BRIDE HAS ESCAPED
by Raye Morgan

#893 A GROOM FOR RED RIDING HOOD
by Jennifer Greene

#894 BRIDAL BLUES
by Cathie Linz

Come join the festivities when six handsome
hunks finally walk down the aisle...

only from

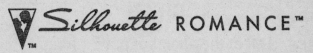
Silhouette ROMANCE™

First comes marriage.... Will love follow?
Find out this September when Silhouette Romance presents

Join six couples who marry for convenient reasons, and still find happily-ever-afters. Look for these wonderful books by some of your favorite authors:

#1030 *Timely Matrimony* by Kasey Michaels
#1031 *McCullough's Bride* by Anne Peters
#1032 *One of a Kind Marriage* by Cathie Linz
#1033 *Oh, Baby!* by Lauryn Chandler
#1034 *Temporary Groom* by Jayne Addison
#1035 *Wife in Name Only* by Carolyn Zane